Warren the 13th *created by* Will Staehle

# Warren the 13th

AND

# THE WHISPERING WOODS

Written by

TANIA DEL RIO

Illustrated & Designed by

WILL STAEHLE

QUIRK BOOKS  PHILADELPHIA

Copyright © 2017 by Will Staehle & Tania del Rio

All rights reserved. No part of this book may be reproduced
in any form without written permission from the publisher.

Library of Congress Cataloging in Publication Number: 2016941166

ISBN: 978-1-59474-929-2

Printed in China

Typeset in Historical Fell Type Roman

Designed by Will Staehle

Illustrations by Will Staehle

Engravings collected by Unusual Corporation and from Shutterstock.com

Production management by John J. McGurk

Warren the 13th is © and a trademark of Unusual Corporation


Quirk Books

215 Church St.

Philadelphia, PA 19106

quirkbooks.com

10 9 8 7 6 5 4 3 2 1

*For Hanh and Sebastian*

# TABLE of CONTENTS

ENJOY THE RIDE | RIGHT THIS WAY

# CHAPTERS

Deep in the Malwoods was a mile-wide crater known as the Black Caldera, home to all of Fauntleroy's most evil witches. Inside the Caldera were many small and filthy huts constructed of mud and twigs. There were murky watering holes and gardens growing poisonous herbs, and everything was cast into shadow by the crater's high, rocky walls.

In the center of the Black Caldera was a large palace made from many thousands of ancient bones, all twisted and woven together by dark magic. And it was here that Calvina, the queen of the witches, rested upon a chaise lounge, gazing at herself in a hand mirror.

Calvina was very vain. She thought she was the most beautiful witch who had ever lived, and she had lived for a very long time. Calvina blew kisses at her reflection through plump, pouting lips.

Sitting nearby were five witches from the queen's coven. Four were busy studying spell books or brewing potions; the fifth was knitting socks. Also standing nearby were two sap-squatch servants. The tall, shaggy creatures watched helplessly from their posts, with stomachs rumbling. The sap-squatches hadn't enjoyed a good meal in many months.

"Your Royal Darkness!" announced a voice from the doorway. "The morning gazette has arrived!"

A young apprentice entered the chamber, clutching a rolled-up newspaper that smelled of fresh ink. Calvina reluctantly tore her eyes away from her mirror and snatched the paper out of the young girl's hands. Her eyes narrowed as she read:

# The Fauntleroy Times

# WALKING WITH THE WARREN
## MY VISIT TO THE WORLD'S FIRST TRAVELING HOTEL

*A Review by Henry J. Vanderbelly, Hotel and Restaurant Critic*

★★★★★

[OUT OF FIVE STARS]

## IT'S AN EXTRAORDINARY SIGHT!

Since its maiden voyage last autumn, the Warren Hotel can be seen crawling over the landscape like an enormous insect as it treks throughout Fauntleroy. However, few people know that this first-class establishment is managed by a twelve-year-old orphan named Warren the 13th!

# WARREN THE 13TH
*Manager*

Despite his youthful age, and a rather odd and frightful appearance, Warren is a bright and hard-working lad descended from a long line of hoteliers, and he has dedicated his life to the management of this most unusual hotel.

# UNCLE RUPERT
*A Buffoon*

The previous manager, Warren's uncle Rupert, was embarrassingly negligent in his duties. Thankfully, young Warren has revitalized the family business, aided by a capable crew of employees, most notably Chef Bunion, who serves three delightful meals a day. Special praise must be given to his celebrated "pudding cookies"—— imagine warm and gooey cocoa pudding encased in a crispy, chocolatey, outer cookie shell. Absolutely delicious!

# CHEF BUNION
*Chef de Cuisine*

Also on Warren's staff is a creature the likes of which I have never seen. It goes by the moniker "Sketchy" and resembles a sort of giant cephalopod with multiple eyes and eight tentacles. I was frightened when I first discovered the [it works in the kitchen, assisting the Chef with

# "SKETCHY"
*A Mystery!*

meals] but I soon found it to be a charming companion endowed with the intelligence of a well-trained dog.

Holding court in the library is the elderly Mr. Friggs, another longtime resident of the hotel. He offers weekly book discussions and free tutoring sessions for any youngsters on board. He is wise, well read, and a former adventurer; he regaled me with a fascinating tale of battling pirates on the island of Barrakas! Nowadays, he is a bit of a recluse and is rarely spotted outside the library, where he serves as the hotel's chief navigator and cartographer. Every week, he does a fine job of charting a new itinerary, selecting the various "ports of call" that the hotel visits on its march around the country.

## MR. FRIGGS
*Librarian & Tutor*

And then there is the hotel's most mysterious employee: Her name is Beatrice, and she serves as Chief of Security, though often she can be found with her violin entertaining guests in the viewing parlor. It would be easy to mistake Beatrice as a member of a traveling circus, for her skin is covered in hundreds of rose tattoos! But don't let the lovely flowers fool you. I'm told she is a legendary witch hunter known as a "perfumier," and each bloom represents just one of the many evil witches she has captured.

## BEATRICE
*Chief of Security*

As for the hotel itself, some guests have remarked on the dark and rather eerie atmosphere of the interior, which is filled with many winding corridors and spooky passageways. I'll confess to getting lost more than once. If you are sensitive to noise, its clanging footsteps might seem distracting on your first visit.

In my estimation, however, these are minor quibbles. The Warren Hotel offers an attentive staff, beautiful vistas, fine dining, and varied company. It is a most marvelous place, indeed!

## "BEATRICE the BOLD"

she hissed. "I've found you at last!" A crazed expression crossed Calvina's face, and she rose to her feet. "Pay attention, girls! If we find this hotel, we can capture Beatrice and avenge all of our sisters she's captured over the years! We'll smash the bottles they're trapped in and free them all!"

The other witches cackled with glee before they remembered that Beatrice was the most feared perfumier of all time. They liked the idea of having her in their clutches . . . as long as another capturer did the clutching.

"Post a bounty throughout the Malwoods!" the queen ordered. "I want Beatrice, her bottles, and her amazing walking hotel!"

"The hotel, too?" asked Calvina's young

That's right! I need a new palace!" the queen declared. "A building like that walking hotel would be the most fearsome palace in the land! I could use it to stomp villages! I could take over the world!"

"Most excellent, Your Royal Darkness," the apprentice said, taking notes on parchment with a quill. "And what kind of bounty will you offer?"

The queen smiled and gazed back into her hand mirror.

## "WHATEVER THE HEART DESIRES."

This promise captured the attention of every witch present in the chamber. They exchanged hungry glances, practically falling over one another as they hurried out the door, eager to be the first to earn th

# CHAPTER 1

## IN WHICH THE

# WARREN STUMBLES

familiar to him as the gentle ticking of a grandfather clock.

Warren knelt on the hotel roof, repairing a broken tile with a hammer and nails. The six crows who lived in the rooftop birdhouse poked their heads out of its windows, croaking for food. Warren set down his hammer and removed a sketchbook from his pocket; he always kept a few slices of cheese tucked between its pages. He tossed them to the birds, who promptly began squabbling over the pieces.

"Share, share!" Warren admonished. "There's enough for everyone."

The crows were lazy and wouldn't leave the birdhouse to search for their own food, but Warren didn't mind. He enjoyed caring for each and every guest of his hotel, even the ones with feathers.

As the birds ate, Warren leaned back against the chimney and flipped through

t was a warm summer afternoon, and the Warren Hotel trundled over the countryside upon its enormous metal legs. The steady *CLANG! CLANG! CLANG!* of its footfalls were loud enough to be heard for miles, but Warren the 13th hardly noticed; the deafening din had become as comforting and

his sketchbook. Its pages were filled with charcoal drawings: doodles of his friends and family at the hotel, and portraits of the fantastic landscapes he'd seen on his travels. But Warren had no time for sketching today; there were too many other problems demanding his attention. He turned to a fresh page and began jotting down a lengthy to-do list, based on all the calls to the front desk he'd received that morning:

ROOM 304
*Small leak in bathroom ceiling.*
ROOM 404
*Large leak in bathroom ceiling.*
ROOM 504
*Giant leak in bathroom ceiling.*
ROOM 604
*Overflowing toilet; water won't turn off.*

Warren was very busy, yet he had no complaints. In fact, he felt like the luckiest boy on earth. He ran the world's first—and only—traveling hotel, and it was so popular that every room was filled! On top of that, the hotel was generating so much money that Warren was finally able to make some much-needed improvements to the antiquated structure. He'd installed a viewing room lined with panoramic windows for the guests to enjoy the scenery as the hotel went along its way. He also added a large window to the control room, so he no longer had to rely on a tiny periscope to navigate the terrain.

Perhaps the biggest advancement was a hidden feature that Warren had discovered inside the control room. It turned out that one of his ancestors, Warren the 2nd, had had a few tricks up his sleeve when he designed the walking hotel, including a special autopilot feature. This option ensured that the hotel would dutifully continue along the road following the precise coordinates input by Warren each morning. Placing the hotel on autopilot spared Warren from having to drive the hotel all day long. Instead, he had the freedom to roam about, mingle with guests, and head up to the roof to repair broken tiles and make to-do lists.

Suddenly, Warren's concentration was broken by the sound of a sputtering engine and a *HONK! HONK! HONK!* He dropped down on his hands and knees and scrambled to the edge of the roof. Far below, an odd-looking automobile was weaving dangerously between the hotel's enormous legs. It had oversized wheels and was painted in garish colors. Its carriage

was cluttered with crates, bags, and jugs. On the side were fancy, curlicue letters proclaiming:

SLY'S MIRACLE ELIXIRS, TINCTURES, AND CORDIALS

The car continued to honk as it screeched around the hotel's crashing footfalls. "Be careful!" Warren yelled, even as he realized that yelling was pointless; the car had already passed the hotel and was now branching off the main road, following a dustier and narrower path that offered a direct route to the Malwoods. Warren watched until he couldn't see the car anymore, wondering why anyone would drive toward such a spooky place.

Over the past few months, Warren had piloted the hotel to many unusual destinations, but one place he swore he'd never go was the Malwoods—a shadowy and twisted forest teeming with witches and other, even more dangerous creatures. Because Warren took the safety of his guests very seriously, he hesitated to travel within five miles of the Malwoods. He opened his sketchbook and added yet another item to his to-do list: Rewire autopilot to avoid this intersection altogether.

He had barely finished writing when the air beside him shimmered. A swirling portal materialized, and out stepped his best friend, Petula. She wore a grave expression. Behind her the pool of silvery-looking liquid vanished.

"The guest in Room 204 just called to complain," she said. "Something about a leaky ceiling."

Warren sighed. "Sometimes I wish there were two of me," he admitted.

He tucked away his sketchbook and Petula helped him to his feet. The first time Warren had met Petula, he'd mistaken her for a ghost. She always dressed entirely in white, and her skin was so pale that it looked nearly translucent. He'd since learned that this was just one of her many unusual traits, along with her ability to draw magical pathways between short distances. She was a young perfumier-in-training, and she was learning the fine art of witch capturing from her mother, Beatrice.

Petula glanced down at Warren's to-do list. "Maybe you should hire a maintenance person," she suggested. "So you don't have to do everything yourself."

Warren shook his head. "My dad always said that a good manager doesn't sit behind a desk and bark orders. A good manager pitches in and helps with the dirty work." He grimaced. "Even if it means unclogging a toilet."

"You might be taking your father's advice a bit too literally," Petula said.

"Maybe," Warren said, "but someone has to do the work."

Tucking his sketchbook in his pocket, Warren started to stand up but lost his balance, landing with a hard thump.

"Ow!" Warren cried. He felt as if the roof had slipped out from under him.

Petula looked alarmed. "What was that?" But before Warren could answer, the hotel lurched again, harder, and this time Warren fell face-first. He realized he was rushing forward—in fact, the entire hotel was rushing forward. Warren scrabbled against the slick tiles, trying to grab something—anything—but his fingers were too short to get a good grip. He found himself sliding on his belly, headed for the edge of the roof. And so was Petula!

"Warren!" she cried.

Warren's stomach flipped as he picked up speed. The edge of the roof zoomed toward him—but there, at the end of the tiles, was a skinny tin gutter. If he timed it just right . . .

Squeezing his eyes shut, Warren flung out an arm. His fingers met metal. He grabbed hard. And he held on tight.

Warren opened his eyes just in time to see Petula tumbling past him. Her hand missed the gutter by inches, but at the very last moment she managed to grasp Warren's ankle.

"Hold on!" he yelled. He saw Petula dangling from his foot by one hand, the ground rushing up behind her. "Because here comes the—"

And with that, the building smashed into the earth with a loud crash.

Somehow, the hotel had fallen.

"Are you okay?" called Petula.

"I—I think so," Warren called back. Clouds of dust rose around them and the air was eerily still. Warren's arms started to shake from the effort of holding on to the gutter.

The weight on his ankle disappeared and a portal materialized on the side—well, now the top—of the hotel. Out jumped Petula. She grabbed Warren by both wrists and yanked him upright next to her.

"What happened?" he said.

"I think the hotel tripped," Petula said. She looked even paler than usual.

"Tripped?" Warren said. "But that's impossible!" In the past six months, the hotel had marched up hillsides, forded streams, and crossed chasms, all without a single misstep. "There are seven different safety features to keep the hotel from falling over!"

"Well, all seven of them must have failed," said Petula, "because the hotel fell right on its face. See?" She pointed at their feet.

Sure enough, instead of the roof, Warren's shoes were resting on a pane of glass—a window! On the other side, two angry guests lay crumpled on the floor—well, actually the wall, which was now the floor—shaking angry fists in his direction.

"We'd better get to the control room," Warren said.

"Do you want me to draw a portal?" Petula asked.

"No, thanks." Ordinarily, a portal would be welcome, since the control room was all the way down in the basement. But after falling and rolling off the side of the building, Warren was way too dizzy for the head-spinning side effects of magical travel. "Let's take the long way."

Of course, the long way was now extra

long, thanks to the topsy-turvy state of the hotel. Carefully, Warren picked his way over to the window of his attic bedroom, sliding it open and dropping through the gap as if it was a trap door. He landed with both feet on a wall he'd decorated with sketches and drawings. When he realized he was standing on one of his favorite illustrations, he quickly hopped off.

Petula climbed down after him, then looked around in astonishment. "Weird!"

It *was* weird. Normally, Warren accessed his bedroom through a trap door in the floor, but now the trap door was in the middle of a wall. Warren pulled it open like a porthole, pushed himself up, and wriggled his way headfirst to the other side. The long hallway was familiar but mixed-up, with doors in the ceiling, doors in the floor, and miniature chandeliers dangling from either side of the trap door like a pair of earrings. Warren felt dizzy and confused just looking at them.

Clearly he wasn't the only one. Behind the floor-doors and the ceiling-doors, Warren could hear the muffled voices of guests. And they were not happy.

"What's going on?" one angry man shouted.

"Just a tiny mishap," Warren answered back.

"How do we get out of here?" cried a woman's voice.

"Stay in your room, ma'am," Petula advised. "We'll be up and running in just a few minutes."

Warren gulped. He certainly hoped that was true.

Above them, between the ceiling-doors, was the gap that led to the grand staircase, which descended through each of the eight levels of the hotel. Normally, Warren could ride the bannister all the way down to the lobby, but gravity was no longer on his side. They'd have to find another way.

"We can take the elevator," Petula said.

"But it hasn't worked in years," Warren said.

"Exactly!" Petula replied.

Warren realized what Petula meant. With the hotel now lying on its side, the elevator shaft was the most direct route from the top floor to the lobby. He took off for the end of the hallway, carefully jumping over the doors and wall sconces under his feet.

The doors were closed, as always, and a sign on the front said:

OUT OF SERVICE
*Our apologies for the inconvenience.*
— MGMT.

Warren had written the words himself, using his best handwriting. He'd been especially proud to sign it "Mgmt.," knowing that he was the one doing the managing these days. But now the sign had to come off. He removed it carefully, then rolled up his sleeves. "We're going to have to pry it open."

Petula nodded, and together she and Warren wiggled their fingers into the seam between the doors. With a great groaning creak, the two heavy panels grated apart, one rolling up and the other disappearing down. Inside, the elevator shaft was very dark.

"You first," Warren said, hoping he sounded polite rather than scared.

Petula went ahead, ducking quickly out of sight.

"Wow!" came her voice. Warren scrambled after her. The elevator shaft was chilly and smelled like axle grease. They picked their way down—or, Warren supposed, across—toward the lobby. Pipes, pulleys, chains, and gears crowded their footsteps, and the only light came from thin strips that shone through the doors at every floor they passed. After counting down from eight, they reached the final set of doors. With a mighty push—and help from Petula—Warren wrenched the doors open and tumbled forward into the lobby.

"Oh dear," Petula said.

Rubbing his head, Warren rose to his feet. Oh dear was right. The lobby—the grand entrance to the Warren Hotel, the first thing that guests saw upon arriving and the last thing they saw before they left—was in utter chaos. The stately potted plants had tipped over, spilling dirt everywhere. The curtains had slid off their rods and lay lumped in the corner of the room like sad velvety ghosts. The lobby desk had overturned, its papers scattered across the ground. The grand chandelier hung limply from the side of the room, opposite the checkered tile floor that was now acting as the wall.

"This is going to require a lot of cleanup," Petula observed.

Warren almost sighed but stopped short. No true manager would ever act so unprofessionally. "Let's check the kitchen," he said. "I want to make sure everyone's okay."

If the lobby was chaos, the kitchen was an absolute disaster. Every pot, pan, utensil, and ingredient that wasn't secured had tumbled to the wall that Warren was now standing on. Splattered eggs and a soupy stew were dripping down the ceiling. At first, Chef Bunion and his assistant, Sketchy, were nowhere to be found. But after Warren hoisted himself into the room—and Petula after him—he found one of Sketchy's tentacles wiggling under a tangle of cookware, apples, potatoes, and canned goods. Chef Bunion, it turned out, was buried under a mound of flour.

"No worries, my boy!" Chef said, clapping the white dust off his apron after Warren dug him out. "We'll get this mess sorted out in no time."

Sketchy let out a weak whistle that didn't sound nearly as certain.

"Oh, come now," Chef said. "I've been meaning to rearrange the kitchen anyway!"

"Well, whatever you need, I'll be back to help," Warren said. "But first I have to get to the control room, so we can get the hotel back on its feet."

They hurried through the basement to the secret passageway that led to the control room. At the end of the passage, Warren could just make out the doors lying open, likely from the crash.

"That looks bad," Petula said.

And it only got worse. Inside the room,

the air snapped with hissing and crackling from what seemed like every part of the hotel's navigation machinery. Sparks leapt from the control panel, which was now hanging upside down. Tendrils of smoke curled out from between buttons, levers, and knobs. The candy-colored lights, usually lively and bright, flickered dimly.

"Oh no!" Warren cried, running his hands through his hair. "How could this happen? Uncle Rupert was supposed to be in charge of the controls . . ."

"Warren?" said a voice. "Is that you?"

Even though the room was nearly pitch black—the windows now rested on the ground outside—there was just enough light to reveal the guilty expression on Uncle Rupert's face.

"What happened?" Warren asked.

"How should I know?" his uncle exclaimed innocently. Ever since relinquishing management of the hotel to Warren, he had taken to dressing far more casually than his usual suit and tie; currently he was sporting beach attire, complete with a sun hat and sandals, no doubt anticipating the next scheduled stop in the seaside town of Shellby. "There I was, just minding my own business, resting in my hammock and trying to enjoy a cold drink, when suddenly out of nowhere a giant moth flew in my cup!"

"I don't understand . . . ," Warren said.

Rupert puffed himself up to his full height, which was still not particularly tall. "Well, I was simply so frightened that

I threw my drink across the room. And I suppose it might have landed on the control panel—"

Warren took a closer look at the array of buttons, levers, and knobs. Sure enough, a syrupy liquid dripped over its sides. Warren reached out a finger, but a spark sizzled at him and he quickly pulled it back.

"But you know the control panel can't get wet!" Warren exclaimed.

"I wasn't drinking water," Rupert said. "I happened to have been enjoying a pineapple sarsaparilla. Anyway, tell me something, Warren. Why is everything so lopsided? It's making me dizzy!"

Petula drew herself a portal. "I'll go get a soapy rag from the supply room."

"Wait—" Warren said, but before he could stop her she had disappeared. His frustration growing, he turned back to his uncle. "I'm announcing a new rule, Uncle Rupert: No more drinks in the control room. Water or otherwise!"

"But—but—" Uncle Rupert stammered, gesturing to the hammock that had been strung from wall to wall but now drooped from the ceiling. "Where else will I be able to enjoy my daily sarsaparilla?"

"Anyplace but here!" Warren said.

Uncle Rupert pouted. "I say we ought to address the moth problem before making any new rules."

Fortunately, just then another portal materialized and Petula reappeared, soapy rag in hand. "A lot of upset guests have made it to the lobby," she said. "I'll try to clean the panel while you go talk to them."

"No!" Warren snapped, snatching the rag from Petula. "Weren't you listening? Cleaning it isn't going to work—the control panel is too delicate."

Petula scowled. "I was only trying to help."

Warren felt a twinge of shame. "I'm sorry," he said. "I'd better get to the lobby and see to the guests."

Petula drew him a portal, and this time Warren didn't object. He stepped into the vortex, and after a twisty sensation that made his stomach feel inside out, he emerged into the lobby, which was now packed full of angry people. As soon as they caught sight of Warren, everyone began complaining:

"What took you so long?"

"Why has the hotel tipped over?"

"I sprained my wrist when I fell!"

"This stop isn't listed on the itinerary!"

"What a horribly jarring experience!"

"This hotel feels like a fun house, but I'm not having any fun at all!"

Warren hurried over to the desk and flipped it upright. "I apologize for the inconvenience, ladies and gentlemen, it's just a small technical difficulty! We'll be on our way shortly."

"I paid a lot of money to stay in a moving hotel," one guest blustered. "What's the point if it's not even moving?"

"Exactly!" another guest chimed in. "I'm checking out, and I demand a full refund!"

Warren blanched. "But we're miles from the next town. There's nowhere to go!"

The guests shouted back their complaints in unison:

"I'd rather walk all day than spend one more moment here!"

"I have a bruise the size of a grapefruit!"

"How am I supposed to sleep when my bed is upside down?"

"I'm checking out, too! And I want my money back!"

Warren did his best to placate his disgruntled clientele and convince them otherwise, but they were beyond reason. A line began to form behind the counter—with, Warren noticed in dismay, a visiting journalist named Mr. Vanderbelly lurking nearby to record every detail on his ever-present notepad.

"Please tell me you're not going to write about this," Warren said to him.

"A journalist must record what he sees," Mr. Vanderbelly said, nodding his head mournfully. "Headline: 'The Warren Stumbles! Is This the End of a Fad?' Or how about: 'The Warren Hotel Plummets—Along with Its Profits!'"

Warren groaned. There was no way around it: he would have to start handing out refunds.

Within an hour, the lobby was empty . . . and so was the hotel's cash box.

Warren turned to Mr. Vanderbelly. "I suppose you'll be checking out, too?"

"And miss documenting the story of the year?" he said with a guffaw. "I think not!"

Before Warren could reply, a loud *HONK! HONK! HONK!* sounded outside. Curious, he peered out the closest window. His former guests were walking down the road toward the next town, luggage in tow, but their way was being blocked by a strange-looking car—the same vehicle Warren had seen earlier that morning. The driver's-side door flung open and out stepped a barrel-chested man in an ill-fitting purple suit. He had thinning hair, long curled mustachios that twitched like antennae, and spidery legs. Surveying the crowd, he smiled broadly, causing several gold teeth to glint in the sun.

After briefly wrestling with a sideways doorknob, Warren hurried outside, ready to intervene.

"Greetings, travelers!" the man exclaimed. "It appears you're on your way to Pineycones. If anyone's interested in a ride, I'll be happy to drive you . . . for a reasonable fee, of course! My trusty jalopy can seat six passengers, and this opportunity is first-come, first-served. Now hop aboard if you'd like to make the initial departure!"

All at once, the Warren's former guests began pushing and shoving into the car. Somehow ten people managed to squeeze their way into six seats. Those remaining looked put out.

"Don't worry, don't worry!" the man said smoothly. "I'll happily make extra trips for paying customers!"

Warren shook his head. He hated to see anyone taking advantage of his guests. Except that they weren't his guests anymore. They had checked out, and until he could get the hotel up and walking again, Warren was out of luck. With a heavy heart, he climbed back into the lobby, the front doors falling closed behind him.

"Mr. Warren!" Mr. Vanderbelly called, waving his pen in the air. "A few questions about your most recent failure!"

"Maybe later," Warren said with a sigh. "First, I need to call an emergency meeting."

he keeper of the Sundry Shoppe waited behind the counter. He was a tall man with gray hair, about seventy years old. In his hand was a canteen that should have cost only a florin or two, but he was trying to convince a customer that it was worth ten times as much.

"Twenty florins seems rather expensive," the customer said.

"But this is no ordinary canteen!" the shopkeeper exclaimed. "It is equipped with a special cap that keeps the water from leaking out."

The customer seemed confused. "All canteens have caps. That's the whole point of a canteen—"

Undeterred, the shopkeeper talked over him. "And imagine how thirsty you'll be without a canteen! It would be irresponsible to leave this store without one. Do you know how far you'll have to walk to find a freshwater spring?"

"Well," the customer said, "there's a freshwater spring just up the road. I travel this way often, and I know these parts fairly well."

The shopkeeper cringed. His store was strategically placed miles away from anything; most customers walked through the door feeling lost, disoriented, and desperate to buy much-needed items.

Apparently this customer was the exception to the rule.

"Fine," the shopkeeper said, chucking the canteen behind the counter. "If that's the case, how much would you like to pay?"

"Two florins," the customer said.

But before the shopkeeper could reply, a deafening crash ended their negotiations. He grabbed a pair of binoculars off the shelf and hurried outside, his annoying customer trailing behind.

Outside, the shopkeeper raised the binoculars and peered through the lenses; over the tops of the trees, he glimpsed the edge of a curious-looking building as well as two long mechanical legs flailing helplessly in the air.

"Must be that walking hotel," the customer said. "I suppose it tripped."

"A walking hotel?" The shopkeeper adjusted the focus on his binoculars. Indeed, it seemed like the building had fallen, and now it was struggling to regain its footing. Something about the structure looked familiar . . .

The annoying customer tugged on the shopkeeper's shirtsleeve. "Look, can I buy the canteen or not?"

"Fine, fine, give me the two florins," the shopkeeper said. At this point, selling junk to tourists was the least of the man's concerns. A bigger opportunity was to be had here— a chance to profit from the wreck of an entire hotel. Hundreds of stranded visitors might be arriving on his doorstep at any moment!

As soon as the customer set off, the shopkeeper morphed from his present state—a tall, gray-haired man—into his true form—a wrinkled imp with small yellow eyes and pointy claws. The seventy-year-old "shopkeeper" was just one of his many disguises. He was a mimic, a creature imbued with the power to transform itself into anyone it encountered. All the mimic needed was the single tooth of a victim and its body would automatically fill in the rest. The mimic crept behind the counter, ready to sell overpriced food and water to stranded passengers. But then he glimpsed a poster that had arrived earlier in the week, and at last he understood why the hotel looked so familiar. Here at last was a chance to have everything his heart desired!

# WANTED

## I
## HEREBY
## DECREE

THAT ANYONE WHO DELIVERS THIS **HOTEL** TO THE BLACK CALDERA SHALL RECEIVE THEIR HEART'S GREATEST DESIRE.

I.

AN ADDITIONAL REWARD SHALL BE ISSUED TO ANYONE WHO DELIVERS THE FAMED PERFUMIER KNOWN AS **BEATRICE THE BOLD**

II.

ALL OTHER RESIDENTS OF THE HOTEL ARE EXPENDABLE

—HER ROYAL DARKNESS
## QUEEN CALVINA

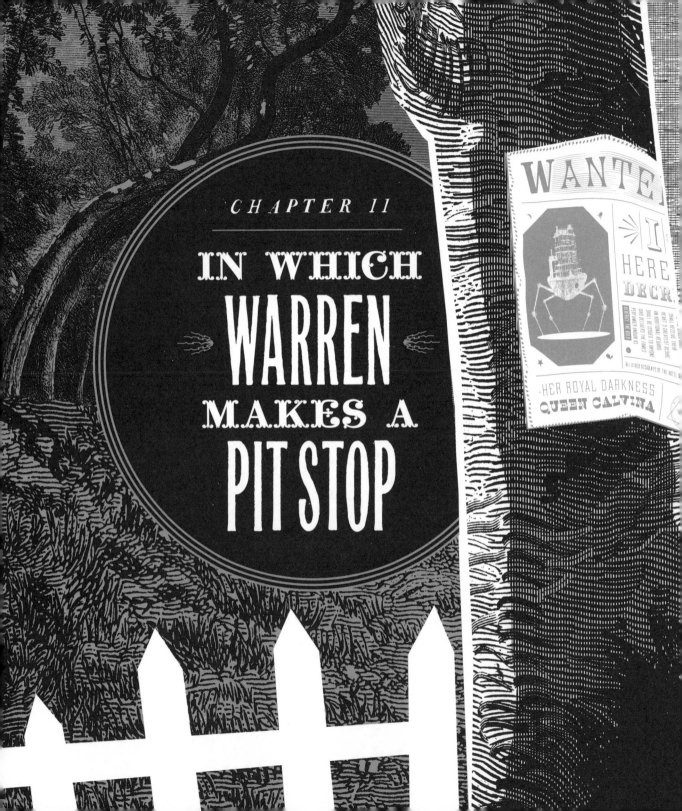

# CHAPTER II

## IN WHICH
### WARREN
## MAKES A
### PIT STOP

**WANTED**

HERE
DECR.

-HER ROYAL DARKNESS
**QUEEN CALVINA**

arren used the hotel intercom to summon his staff, urging everyone to gather in the ballroom. The largest space in the hotel, it also served as the dining hall. Crystal chandeliers hung limply from the west wall, casting a dim flickering light across the overturned table. Normally the table was grand enough to seat fifty guests, but now it resembled a centipede flipped on its back, lying helpless with its legs in the air.

Within moments, Mr. Friggs, Chef Bunion, Sketchy, Beatrice, Petula, and Uncle Rupert had assembled as requested. [Mr. Vanderbelly slipped inside as well, notebook and pen at the ready.] With everyone's help, Warren managed to flip the dining table right side up, and then each person extracted a chair from the jumbled pile in the corner of the room.

"That's a little better, thank you," Warren said, taking a seat. "Now, it seems that our first order of business is repairing the control panel."

"What happened to the control panel?" Mr. Friggs said.

Warren glanced at his uncle, carefully choosing his next words: "There was an unfortunate incident with a pineapple sarsaparilla, which caused the machinery to malfunction." As Warren spoke, his uncle slumped so low in his chair that he was practically under the table.

"This is a disaster!" Mr. Friggs exclaimed, his pale eyes blinking behind round spectacles. "Rebuilding the control panel will take weeks, possibly months!"

"We don't need to rebuild it," said Chef Bunion, a stout fellow with a sharp beak-like nose and arms as big as ham hocks. "All we need is a little Dr. Stickler's De-Stickifier! I've used it on the gooiest pots and pans and it works like a dream!"

Sketchy whistled, his bulbous head nodding in agreement.

"I used our last bottle of De-Stickifier

a week ago," Warren said with a frown. "I needed to dissolve the wads of chewing gum under the third-floor billiards table. And now we're stranded too far from the next town to get any more."

"I wish my portals worked over longer distances," Petula said. Her magic could be quite convenient in a hurry, but a portal would take them only so far: about one hundred feet, to be exact, slightly less on rainy afternoons.

Beatrice held up a card—*fwip!*—engraved with a post box. It was her sole means of communication: many years earlier, an evil witch had stolen her voice, and now she was forced to communicate using flash cards.

"Mom's right—we could order some by mail!" Petula said.

"That will take too long," Warren countered.

"We don't have a choice," Chef Bunion said.

"Hold on a moment," interjected Mr. Friggs, the hotel's chief navigator. He pulled a map from his pocket and unfolded it across the table. "We may be far from the next town, but if I recall ... A-ha!" He jabbed at the map with a knobby finger. "There it is. A tiny general store not too far

from here. Just ten minutes down the road. Perhaps it's worth a look?"

Warren's heart leapt a little. Perhaps, indeed!

"I'll go right now!" Warren said. "With any luck we can fix the hotel and reach Pineycones by the end of the day. If we catch up to the guests, I'm sure I can convince them to give us another try."

Petula turned to her mother. "Can I go with him?"

Beatrice riffled through her deck of cards again—*fwip!*—and held out a card engraved with a caution sign: Be careful.

Petula patted the pocket where she kept a perfumier bottle, her tool for capturing a witch. "Don't worry, Mom. If anything happens, I'll be ready."

Sketchy tried to follow his master to the exit, but Warren urged him to stay behind. "Sorry, Sketchy," he said, "but I'm not sure if this store allows pets. It's best if you stay here."

"Come on, Sketch," Chef Bunion called, "back to the kitchens! There's still lunch that needs preparing! And if you're good, maybe Warren will bring you back a piece of candy."

Sketchy whistled happily and clapped its tentacles as it followed Chef Bunion back toward the kitchen. Uncle Rupert turned to Warren with a pleading look. "Will you bring me back a piece of candy, too?"

Warren sighed. "I'll try."

Gravity kept Warren from exiting through the front door, so instead he opened a window near the back of the hotel, climbed outside, and dropped the five feet to the ground below. A moment later, Petula magically appeared beside him.

The land outside the hotel was desolate. The guests were gone, already traveling on foot or by car to Pineycones. Wide-open prairie stretched as far as the eye could see, waving with dry grass and spotted with pale and thirsty trees. Random clusters of boulders sat piled here and there, as though dropped by a careless giant. Miles ahead loomed the Malwoods, dark and menacing. Warren shivered every time he looked at the forbidding line of trees that marked its border.

Warren and Petula walked quickly along the road, and soon they came to a thicket of hedges and a wooden hand-painted sign that read:

JUST AHEAD!

## The SUNDRY SHOPPE

DELICIOUS FOOD
REFRESHING BEVERAGES
ESSENTIAL TRAVEL SUPPLIES
EMERGENCY & COSMETIC DENTISTRY

OPEN 24 HOURS

"Emergency and cosmetic dentistry?" Warren said.

"Seems like an odd specialty," Petula agreed.

As they passed through the hedges, the building revealed itself. It looked charming enough, with a log-cabin facade and a rustic porch that held a variety of comfortable rocking chairs. There was even a barrel with a checkerboard on top, the game pieces arranged for a new set of players.

Warren and Petula clomped up the wooden steps to the screen door that served as the shop's entrance. When they pushed it open, bells jingled merrily.

The shelves were so full of merchandise that there was scarcely enough room for Warren and Petula to step inside. The Sundry Shoppe seemed to carry everything a traveler might need: giant cans of food sat alongside hammers, cookware, and rain ponchos. On the floor were sleeping bags and canvas tents, canteens and grappling hooks, not to mention an entire section full of wind-up toy monkeys.

Petula studied them. "Why would travelers need a—"

"Hello there!" cried a cheerful voice, and a kindly old man tottered over to greet them. "Welcome to the Sundry Shoppe! Can I help you find something?"

"Any chance you have Dr. Stickler's De-Stickifier?" Warren asked.

"Of course I do!" the shopkeeper said. "Right this way!"

The man led Warren and Petula through a maze of aisles. Eventually they arrived at a glass case filled with De-Stickifier, more than a hundred bottles in all different sizes. "You have so many!" Warren exclaimed.

"It's very popular round these parts," the shopkeeper explained. "Because of all the sap, you see."

"What sap?" Warren asked.

"The Malwoods are full of pine trees," the shopkeeper explained. "Thousands of trees, maybe tens of thousands. During peak season, the sap was everywhere. Heck, I used to harvest it for recipes. Tastes just like cotton candy!"

Warren's stomach rumbled. After a morning spent working on the rooftop and refunding money to angry guests, he realized that he had completely forgotten to eat lunch. "That sounds delicious," he said dreamily.

"Unfortunately, we have a shortage right now," the shopkeeper continued. "About six months ago, for some mysterious reason no one knows, all of the pine trees went dry. So suddenly I've got plenty of De-Stickifier!"

"Lucky me," Warren said, grabbing three bottles.

"I'm not sure if you'll be interested," the man continued, "but I also have some sap candy."

"Candy!" Warren and Petula exclaimed in unison.

They followed eagerly as the shopkeeper led them across the store and into yet another aisle, where an assortment of confections and treats was displayed in enticing and colorful rows. Warren and Petula rushed forward. Their eyes were drawn to a chocolate bar called Choco-Sap Crunch and a packet of cookies called Sappy-Chip Cookies and a fruity-looking taffy called Happy Sappy Taffy.

"Go ahead. Try a piece!" the shopkeeper said.

Warren unwrapped a piece of squishy chocolate called Sap-Mallow Surprise and popped it in his mouth. Sugary sweetness flooded his senses. "It really does taste like cotton candy!"

"Oh, yes, it's heavenly," the shopkeeper said. "The only downside is that it rots your teeth so quickly."

# "Excuushme?"

Warren asked, still chewing.

"Yes, something toxic in the sap; it's very hard on the tooth's enamel. Melts the bone like acid. But no worries! I happen to be a professional dentist, so I can solve the problem lickety-split."

"Couldn't you have warned us?" Petula asked. "We have a hotel to fix!"

"It won't take long, young lady. A mere ten minutes. You're welcome to wait here while I treat your friend to a cleaning."

Warren shook his head. He finished chewing and swallowed hard. "There's no time. Petula, why don't you take the De-Stickifier back to the hotel, and I'll catch up when we're finished."

"Oh, fine," Petula said, glaring one last time at the shopkeeper. "But you really should put a warning label on those sap candies!"

The shopkeeper smiled kindly, then put a hand on Warren's shoulder and ushered him toward the back room. Warren had never seen a dentist's office before; it resembled the hotel's infirmary, with cabinets of

medical supplies and a single large reclining chair in the center.

"Go on now," the shopkeeper said. "Take a seat and I'll strap you in."

"Strap me in?" Warren asked, easing himself onto the chair.

"Oh, yes, mustn't be too careful," the man said, laughing merrily. He pulled strap after strap over Warren's chest and legs, yanking them taut and buckling them into place. "We can't have you thrashing about when I perform the extraction!"

"Extraction?" Warren asked. "I thought you said this was a cleaning!"

"They're practically the same thing," the shopkeeper said.

He closed the door to the shop and then stepped to the nearest window. Out on the path, he saw Petula walking back toward the hotel; she curved around a cluster of trees, vanishing out of sight. Satisfied, the shopkeeper turned back to Warren.

"Now there's no need to worry," he said. "I just need one tooth. I'll even take it from the back of your mouth, so no one shall ever notice!"

"What are you talking about?" Warren asked. "You said I needed a cleaning! Because the sap would ruin my teeth!"

"I'm afraid that was an exaggeration. Your teeth will be just fine," the shopkeeper confided. "But if I'm to mimic you properly, I need to borrow one. That's how my magic works." And with that the shopkeeper reached for a pair of metal forceps. "Once my transformation is complete, I will walk back to your hotel and seize control. Then I'll deliver the hotel to the Black Caldera, where Queen Calvina has promised me an extraordinary reward!"

"No!" Warren cried. He wrestled against the leather bindings, but it was no use. He was trapped!

"Open wide," the shopkeeper said, clicking his forceps.

Warren braced himself for a terrible pain, but to his surprise, the shopkeeper tugged gently and the tooth popped out of his mouth without the slightest pain. The man raised the forceps to the sunlight streaming through the window, and the yellow tooth shone like a prized jewel.

"Excellent!" he rasped. Then he took the tooth in his fingers and pushed it inside his mouth. Warren's disgust was quickly replaced by astonishment as the shopkeeper's form flickered and faded amid a swirl of shadowy magic. Within seconds, the elderly man was transformed into an exact clone of Warren the 13th!

"Who are you?" Warren asked.

# CALL ME WORRIN!

**WARREN'S DOUBLE SAID,** laughing in a voice that sounded exactly like his own. "But it will be best if you don't say anything. Just sit tight and relax." And before Warren could say or do anything, the mimic stuffed a wad of cotton balls into his mouth. "I must be off. I'm going to take your hotel for a little stroll!"

"No!" Warren tried to cry out, but the word was muffled by his mouthful of cotton. Worrin walked out the door of his shop. Seconds later, Warren watched as the impostor passed by the window of the dentistry office, heading up the road toward the hotel.

*Toward* my *hotel*, Warren thought. And though he struggled and thrashed to break free once again, the bindings refused to budge. There was no escape.

47

CHAPTER III

IN WHICH
WORRIN
VISITS THE
WARREN

s Worren approached the hotel, he realized he didn't know the best way to enter. Going through the front door wasn't an option, not with the building still toppled on its side. Instead he approached the nearest first-floor window, pushed it open, and climbed through.

Unexpectedly, he found himself in some kind of pantry. Dozens of wooden shelves had collapsed onto the "floor." Everywhere he stepped were cans and jars and boxes of food, as if the room's contents had been scrambled by a tornado. Worren hoisted open the door, then dropped down into the hallway below. The corridor was strangely deserted.

*If this hotel is so popular,* he thought, *then where are all the guests?*

Worren walked quickly down the hallway, hopping over the occasional doorway, until he encountered a big-bellied man with slicked-back hair and a dazed expression.

"There you are, Warren!" he exclaimed. "Did you bring back any candy for your dear Uncle Rupert?"

The very clever Worren did not miss a trick. "Of course," he said, fishing into his pockets and removing a piece of sap-water taffy. "Here you are, Uncle. I know how much you love taffy!"

Rupert quickly unwrapped the candy and popped it into his mouth. "Itsh shticky!" he said, chewing loudly. "Do you have any more?"

"Yes, but first, it's extremely important that I get to the control room," Worren said. "Unfortunately, I bumped my head climbing back into the hotel, and everything feels so topsy-turvy. I'm a little woozy. Could you help me?"

Uncle Rupert puffed out his chest. Clearly he was flattered by the request; he had so few chances to feel useful anymore. "Why, of course!" he said. "Right this way, my boy. I'm happy to show you the way!"

It soon became clear that Rupert was even more disoriented than Worrin, but it didn't really matter, because Rupert ended up giving Worrin an extended tour of the hotel. They visited the ballroom, the kitchen, the lobby, even a few guestrooms. Along the way, Worrin prompted Rupert with questions, rewarding him with a taffy after every answer. It was rather like training a dog. Rupert lamented that all the guests had fled the hotel, and Worrin did his best to look disappointed as well. "Yes, it's really too bad," he said, but inside he rejoiced. *Perfect,* he thought, *fewer people to worry about!* Worrin learned that someone named Mr. Friggs was in charge of hotel navigation [*that will have to change,* Worrin thought] and there was a perfumier named Beatrice who lived on the eighth floor [*I will have to watch out for her,* Worrin decided].

Eventually they found themselves standing at a closet underneath a staircase, and Rupert began showing Worrin the latest additions to his collection of sarsapa-

rilla bottles. Worrin was pretending to be awestruck when a girl suddenly materialized in front of them. The mimic recognized her from the Sundry Shoppe.

"There you are!" she exclaimed, taking Worrin by the hand. "Where have you been? Chef Bunion and I finished cleaning the control panel and we think it's ready to go."

"Of course!" Worrin said. "I'm sorry to keep you waiting. Lead the way!"

Petula looked at him oddly. "Are you feeling all right?"

Worrin hesitated. "The dentist gave me some laughing gas," he said.

"And he bumped his head," Uncle Rupert added helpfully.

Petula frowned but didn't say anything as she led Worrin through the hotel. Inside the control room, Worrin tried not to gawk at all the wires and cables and lights and buttons. With a twinge of anxiety, he realized he didn't know the first thing about piloting a hotel. Delivering the building to the Black Caldera might be more challenging than he had thought.

A burly man in a greasy apron was waiting for them. Worrin gathered from Rupert's remarks that this must be Chef Bunion, the hotel's head cook and all-around handyman.

"It's as good as new!" Chef Bunion said, slapping the top of the control panel with his meaty hand. "Turn it on and we'll see if that De-Stickifier did the trick."

"All right," Worrin said. He thought it would be a good idea to sit in the pilot's chair, but it was currently sticking sideways out of the wall. Worrin decided to climb up onto the control panel instead. Petula and Chef watched from below, while Rupert busied himself with his broken hammock.

Worrin stared worriedly at the controls. Everyone was watching him, waiting, as the seconds ticked by. It was getting awkward. *Just do something,* he said to himself. So he reached out tentatively and pushed a large green button.

Nothing happened.

"You have to use the activation panel first," Petula said, pointing to a flat square area lined with tiny light bulbs. "Remember?"

"Of course!" Worrin said, slapping his hand on the panel. Without delay, all the lights blinked on and a hum filled the room. Then the entire building began to sway— Worrin felt the floor rising under his feet as the hotel righted itself. He fell back into the pilot's chair as Petula and Chef Bunion grabbed at wires and cables to steady themselves. The giant structure rumbled as it rose on its enormous legs, and light flooded in through the large windows. Worrin stifled a gasp and tried his best not to look as astonished as he felt.

"It works!" Petula said. "We fixed it!"

"Well done!" Chef Bunion said. "Now let's get moving!"

Worrin pressed on a lever, assuming it would make the building step forward—but nothing budged.

"You forgot the passcode," Petula said.

"The what?"

"The hotel won't move unless you enter the code."

"Right, of course!" Worrin said. "I can't believe I forgot to enter the passcode!"

Now he was truly stuck. *How will I figure out the passcode?* Fortunately, he didn't have to. With a sigh, Petula reached past him, placing her fingers on typewriter keys installed in the side of the panel. She proceeded to type, and the panel answered with a cheerful bell tone as the lever unlocked. Worrin again pressed it down, and this time the hotel obeyed, stepping forward with ease. His heart was pounding with excitement, and he couldn't help but release a triumphant laugh. This was too easy! He'd deliver the hotel and collect his reward in no time at all!

Petula noted her friend's strange expression. "Warren, are you sure you're okay?"

"Yes, I'm fine," he said reassuringly. "Just a little crazy from all the excitement."

"Then, to be safe, let's put the hotel on autopilot, okay?"

Again, Petula stepped in and showed him the proper switch, reminding him that the hotel was set on a course for the nearest town—Pineycones.

"Yes, yes, of course," Worrin said. "Thank you for being so patient. I'm quite embarrassed."

"Don't be," Petula said, waving him away. "I'm sure the laughing gas will wear off soon."

"You just need some food!" Chef said. "That will set you right again!"

"Good idea," Petula said. "With all the excitement, we missed lunch."

"Ooh, lunch!" Uncle Rupert said. "Yes, let's eat!"

Worrin followed them out of the control room, stopping once to stare longingly at the control panel. He needed to find a way to change the hotel's course for the Black Caldera without anyone noticing. *I can worry about that later*, he decided. His stomach was rumbling, and a meal sounded rather appealing.

They reached the kitchen, which was filled with fragrant and spicy aromas. As soon as they entered, Chef Bunion went right to work, chopping parsnips and acorn squash with impressive skill and speed. "Help yourself to some pudding cookies," he said, opening a canister and passing it around. Petula eagerly grabbed three cookies, handing one each to Worrin and Rupert.

Worrin bit into his cookie, and gooey chocolate pudding oozed out. He closed his eyes in bliss. The cookie was even more delicious than sap candy!

"Lunch will be ready in ten minutes," Chef said. Then he raised his voice and called, "Sketchy, where are you?"

A door on the opposite side of the kitchen banged open and out popped an enormous, be-tentacled creature carrying a towering stack of pots and pans. The beast resembled a giant octopus, except that it had multiple eyes and wore a white chef's hat upon its bulbous head. Worrin stumbled back in shock. Rupert had mentioned that Warren kept some kind of pet in the hotel, but he didn't expect anything quite like this!

"Hey, Sketchy!" Petula said casually, and the beast chirped a cheerful reply.

*Stay calm*, Worrin thought, though his heart was racing.

"Hello, Sketchy," he said in an effort to recover. *Act natural*, he told himself.

Sketchy froze. Then the beast blinked at Worrin with its many eyes. Then it set down the pots and pans with an angry clatter and rushed toward him, whistling like an angry teakettle. It took all of Worrin's willpower not to flee in terror. The beast used one of its tentacles to yank the cookie from Worrin's hand and slam it back in the canister.

"Sketchy, don't be rude!" Petula said, laughing.

Chef Bunion chuckled. "Sketchy must be

worried you'll spoil your appetite!"

*It doesn't like me!* Worrin thought in a panic. *It can tell I'm not the real Warren!*

Worrin tried his best to laugh. "No, no. Sketchy is absolutely right. I should save room for lunch." He attempted to pat Sketchy's tentacle, but the beast sprang away.

"Sketchy, what's wrong?" Petula asked. "Why are you acting like that?"

In reply, the creature whistled a series of short, frantic bursts. Worrin studied Petula's face and was flooded with relief; she clearly had no idea what it was trying to communicate. Still, Worrin knew that it wouldn't take much for Petula to grow suspicious . . .

"Poor Sketchy," Worrin said. "He must be, um, feeling poorly."

Petula laughed. "He? Warren, you know very well that Sketchy isn't a he!"

"Of course," Worrin said, laughing nervously. "Of course she's not a he!"

Petula stared at him even more closely. "But Sketchy isn't a she, either. Sketchy is just . . . Sketchy!"

Sketchy narrowed its eyes and trilled.

Worrin felt certain he'd been exposed, but fortunately Chef Bunion was quick to intervene. "If Sketchy is sick, it shouldn't be handling food. In fact, it shouldn't be anywhere near the kitchen. The entire hotel could be contaminated!"

"That's right," Worrin said. "We need to consider the safety of our guests!"

Sketchy let out a high-pitched whistle: *No, no, that's not it—*

"Sorry, friend," Chef Bunion continued. "I'll miss your help, but it's for the best."

"Chef is right," Worrin said a little too excitedly. "Sketchy needs to rest. I'll find a nice quiet room where it can be quarantined and everything will be fine."

# "QUARANTINED?"

Petula asked. "But that sounds so severe!"

"It's for the safety and well-being of everyone," Worrin said, grabbing a tentacle and dragging Sketchy out of the kitchen. The beast sputtered a series of helpless chirps, but Petula knew there was no point in arguing. Nothing was more important to Warren than his hotel and its guests.

"Don't worry, Sketchy," Petula called after them. "When we reach the next town, we'll find a doctor who can help you."

Worrin wasted no time pulling the creature down a twisted and turning hallway that led to one of the basement's darkest corners. He opened the door to a cramped and tiny space, apparently some kind of utility closet, whose walls were lined with shelves of cleaning supplies and paint cans.

"In you go!" Worrin said, pushing Sketchy inside. The beast collided with the shelves, sending buckets clattering to the floor. Worrin slammed the door and locked it as Sketchy whistled shrilly from the other side.

"Now behave," Worrin warned, "or I won't bring you any food or water!"

The whistling quieted, and Worrin rubbed his hands together. He felt quite pleased with himself! He had already managed to eliminate the one creature that could see through his disguise; as long as the beast was locked away, it wouldn't be able to warn a soul.

Now for the next challenge: How to get the hotel to...

# CHAPTER IV

## IN WHICH

# WARREN

## MAKES A

# DEAL

eanwhile, back at the Sundry Shoppe, Warren squirmed and stretched and struggled, but the strong leather straps wouldn't budge, not even an inch. He was able, at least, to spit out the cotton. Then he realized, bleakly, that the only way he might escape his bonds was if he didn't eat for days and lost a few pounds. But by then his hotel would be long gone, firmly in the clutches of the evil witches in the Black Caldera.

Warren closed his eyes and breathed slowly, trying to calm himself down. He had to think clearly.

After a few moments wracking his brain for methods of escape, Warren heard the distant sound of an engine. His eyes flicked open and he glanced out the window. Driving up to the shop was the colorful car he'd spotted earlier, the one that had ferried his guests to Pineycones.

*Please stop*, Warren thought desperately. *Please, please, please—*

As if hearing his prayers, the car pulled over to the side of the road. A moment later, Warren heard the jingle of the door leading into the Sundry Shoppe. "Hello, anybody here?" the man called out. "I just made a small fortune driving a bunch of tourists to Pineycones. I need to buy all the reptile food you can spare."

"Help!" Warren yelled as loud as he could. "I'm in the back!"

A moment later the door opened, and the man poked his head inside. "Do you work in the store?"

"Do I look like I work in the store?" Warren asked. "I'm trapped! Can you please set me free?"

The man paused to consider the question. "Well, that depends," he said. "What can you offer me in return?"

Warren was shocked. He never thought he'd have to bargain his way out of this predicament!

"You just made a fortune by stealing all of my hotel guests," Warren said. "Wasn't that enough?"

"I'm afraid not," the man replied calmly.

"Well, I do have a little money," Warren told him.

"How little?"

"Untie me and you can see for yourself."

"Hmph," the man said. "All right. But if you're lying, I'll put you right back in this chair!"

The man unbuckled the straps and Warren spilled out of the chair, grateful to be back on his feet. He rubbed the feeling back into his numb arms; after spending so much time tied up in the chair, they felt like spaghetti noodles.

"Thank you," Warren said.

"Don't thank me yet. Where's the money?"

Warren dug into his pockets and handed over everything he had. He hoped it would be enough. The man squinted down at the wad of bills and sniffed. "Well, it ain't much, but I suppose it'll do."

He turned abruptly and walked back into the shop, with Warren following close behind. The man grabbed a shopping basket and headed to a corner where mini cauldrons and candles were piled high, along with jars of questionable ingredients for spells, like toenail clippings and frogs' spawn. He picked up a container of dried crickets and read the label. "Perfect," he said, and then proceeded to fill his basket.

"Where are you headed?" Warren asked.

"Malwoods," the man grunted. "What's it to you?"

"That's where I'm headed, too!" Warren said. "Can I get a lift?"

"What do I look like, a taxi service?" the man said.

Warren reminded him that he had just driven many of the hotel guests to Piney-cones in exchange for payment, which sounded an awful lot like a taxi service.

"I suppose that's true," the man said. "But you no longer have any money, so there's no reason for me to help you." He knelt down and picked up a jug of fuel. "Now where is that shopkeeper?"

"He's gone," Warren said. "And I don't think he's coming back anytime soon."

"Excellent! Then I guess I'll enjoy a special discount."

Without further ado, the man left the store, the door jingling merrily in his wake. Warren looked longingly out the window as the man sped away in his strange jalopy. He realized that he would have to pursue the hotel on foot.

Fortunately, everything he could possibly need for a long walk through the wilderness was right there in the shop. Warren grabbed a knapsack off the shelf and then wandered through the aisles, gathering anything useful: a compass, a lantern, a canteen, a book of matches, and a small tin pot with a fork and knife clipped to the handle. Digging around, Warren even found a forgotten jar of sap tucked in the back of a shelf, hidden behind cans of baked beans and peas. He uncorked the bottle and sniffed. It smelled sweet and sugary, with a hint of vanilla, just like cake frosting. He decided he would give it to Chef Bunion. Surely a professional cook would know what to do with it.

Even with all the supplies, there was still plenty of room in the knapsack, so Warren went to the candy case and filled the rest of his bag with snacks and a couple bottles of Sappy Cola. Then he shrugged his backpack onto his shoulders, testing its weight. It was heavy, but as the hotel's only bellhop he was

used to ferrying stacks of suitcases up and down stairs, so he knew he could manage just fine.

On his way past the cash register, Warren paused beside a crate filled with rolls of yellow paper: maps! He sorted through until he found one showing the Malwoods. Spreading the map on the counter, Warren studied the landscape. Little green triangles covered the surface, which Warren knew represented trees. A bold wiggly line appeared to depict a wide river, and a dotted line was likely a road. It cut through the heart of the forest, winding this way and that before eventually reaching the farthest edge, where it met the sea. And there, at the limit of the Malwoods, was a crude circle etched with dark lines. Warren didn't need to read the legend to know this was the dreaded Black Caldera. Somehow he would have to catch the hotel before it reached that spot. But how?

Obviously, the hotel walked much faster than Warren did—but he realized that, because of its size, it would be forced to follow the road. This gave Warren an advantage—if he cut through the forest in a straight line, he had a good chance of beating the hotel. Of course, venturing off the road was likely to be extremely dangerous.

BEWARE THE
SAP-SQUATCHES!

LLOW

LLA

ERNS

SPIDER
CRANNY

SMOKE
SLITHER
SWAMP

The map was also speckled with black pointed hats, representing witch villages. These had ominous names like "Wart Hollow" and "Wickedsville" and "Smoke Slither Swamp." Warren certainly didn't want to stumble upon a village of witches.

Warren gave the map one last look. That was when he noticed the most alarming detail of all: a small square in the top right corner. It featured a bizarre depiction of a furry man and was captioned with a dire warning: "Beware the Sap-squatches!" Warren had never heard of a "sap-squatch," and after seeing the illustration, he was certain he didn't want to see one, either.

Feeling as prepared as he could be, Warren rolled up the map, tucked it into his knapsack, and glanced at his pocket watch. It was getting late, with only a few hours of daylight left to guide his way. He wanted to cover as much ground as possible before night fell. So he hurried out of the shop and took a deep breath as he faced the darkening band of trees on the horizon. Then Warren plunged ahead, walking briskly through the tall grass in the direction of the dreaded

# Malwoods . . .

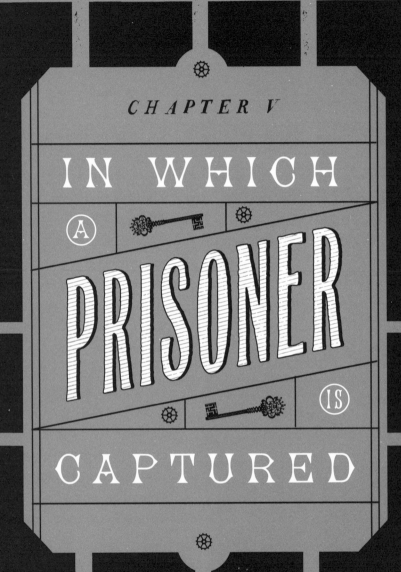

CHAPTER V

IN WHICH

Ⓐ

PRISONER

IS

CAPTURED

etula carried a tray of food to the viewing room on the eighth floor, where her mother liked to spend her free time. What was formerly a dank and stuffy parlor had been transformed by Warren with the addition of panoramic windows on the outer walls. Now light flooded in, making the room appear much airier and more spacious than it really was.

Most days the viewing room was the most popular destination in the hotel, full of guests watching the scenery sail by. So it was rather jarring for Petula to arrive and find the space nearly empty. Now that the guests had left, the only people present were Beatrice [playing a sad song on her violin] and Mr. Vanderbelly, who was seated by the fireplace and immersed in a book.

"I brought some lunch," Petula said, setting the tray on a nearby table.

Her mother smiled gratefully. Mr. Vanderbelly sniffed loudly and said, "That smells delicious! Acorn squash and parsnip potpie, is it?"

Petula nodded, impressed by Mr. Vanderbelly's olfactory senses. "Sketchy appears to be ill," she told her mother. "Warren put it in quarantine."

"Quarantine! How very dramatic!" Mr. Vanderbelly said, reaching into his pocket for a notebook and pen. Petula frowned at his back. She was tired of him always hanging about and listening to conversations that were none of his business.

"It's really not a big deal," she said. "It's probably just a cold."

Beatrice looked concerned and rapidly pulled out a series of picture cards: a question mark, a thermometer, a skull-and-crossbones, a querulous gorilla. Mr. Vanderbelly attempted to eavesdrop but couldn't read the cards as fluently as Petula could.

"I suppose you're right," Petula said to her mother. "I'll check tomorrow."

Beatrice nodded, satisfied that her request would be fulfilled, and then sat down to dine with Mr. Vanderbelly.

Suddenly, the room seemed to flicker with shadows, and a dark blur shot past the windows. The trio hurried to the glass and peered outside. At first, they saw nothing but wide-open prairie and waves of golden grass. But then another shadow flitted by, and another, and another.

# WITCHES! ON BROOMS!

Beatrice's face darkened, and with a *fwip-fwip-fwip!* she flashed a series of cards telling Petula, in no uncertain terms, to stay put. Then she vaulted out of the observation room and into the hallway.

"What did she say?" Mr. Vanderbelly asked worriedly. "Where is she going?"

Petula sprinted for the door. "She's going to fight those witches and she wants us to stay here."

"Then where are you going?" he cried.

"To help her!"

After all, Petula was a perfumier-in-training. Though her mother didn't think she was ready for battle, Petula knew otherwise. Confident in her abilities, she patted the empty bottle in her pocket, knowing she had everything necessary to make her first capture. In the instant any witch tried to use magic, Petula would open the bottle, magically drawing the witch inside.

Petula raced into the hallway but paused at the hotel intercom. "Stop the hotel!" she shouted down to the control room. "We're under attack!" She knew it would be easier to fight on the roof of a stationary hotel than a moving one.

By the time Petula reached the roof, her mother was already surrounded by five witches hovering on brooms. They swooped around her, cackling madly and throwing bolts of lightning and fire. Beatrice leapt and twirled like an acrobat, dodging each attack as the scent of sulfur bloomed in the air. Crouching low to avoid another blast, she uncorked a bottle, and with a *whooosh* the nearest witch was sucked inside, screaming.

"She got Kragga!" snarled one of the remaining witches. "Stop casting spells! That's what allows them to catch us!" She landed on the roof and spun her broom like a stave; the other witches followed in formation. They pressed forward, swinging and stabbing with their wooden handles.

Beatrice fended them off, blocking each thrust with her arms and legs. She overpowered one witch with spiky blue hair and tossed her off the edge of the roof, but the witch used her broom to stop the fall and then swooped back into battle. Beatrice was vastly outnumbered.

"This is truly remarkable!" Mr. Vander-belly exclaimed upon seeing Beatrice's display of prowess. Somehow he had followed Petula onto the roof and was now furiously jotting notes in his notebook.

Petula pushed him away. "Get back!"

She reached for her empty perfume bottle, ready to uncork it the instant a witch cast a spell. Somehow she would have to trick them into using magic. "Hey, stink breath!" she yelled to the closest one, an old crone with spiky pink hair. "Come and get me!"

Upon hearing her daughter's voice, Beatrice's expression turned from determination to horror. She shook her head furiously, and Petula didn't need a picture card to know that her mom was saying "NO!"

But it was too late. Petula had come ready
to fight.

"Well, well, well! What have we here?"
cackled the pink-haired witch. Her hands
glowed neon blue as she prepared to shoot a
spell.

*Here's my chance,* thought Petula.

But just as the witch released a crackling bolt of lightning, Petula fumbled with her bottle and it slipped from her fingers. She glanced up in dismay as the bolt arced toward her with terrifying speed. But with a startling *whoosh!* the witch and her spell were vacuumed into one of Beatrice's bottles.

Now three witches remained. Two rushed forward, seizing Petula. "Let me go!" Petula cried, kicking and fighting, but she was no match for their strength.

Beatrice rushed forward, rage flashing in her eyes, but hesitated when the blue-haired witch yelled, "Stop! Or the little girl gets it!" Then she hooked her broom handle around Beatrice's neck, holding her in place. "Move one muscle, and your little girl's a goner. Got it?"

Beatrice stood still as a stone.

"I'm sorry, Mom!" Petula cried. "I didn't think they'd catch me!"

Before Petula and Beatrice could meet their doom, another figure burst out the door and onto the roof. It was Worrin, and he was running right into the middle of the action.

"What is this madness?" he cried. "Let them go!"

"Shut up, Toadface," yelled one of the witches. "We're bringing Beatrice to the queen and you can't stop us."

"No!" Worrin cried. "She's mine!"

Petula thought that was a strange way for Warren to describe his friendship with her mother, but this was no time to quibble over words. Her friend was risking his life, and Petula needed all the help she could get.

Unfortunately, before Worrin could do any good, the blue-haired witch managed to grab him, too, and then proceeded to drag both children dangerously close to the roof's edge. Petula peered down to the ground far below, and her stomach flipped nervously. There would be no portaling her way out of this trouble, not with the witch's iron grip on her casting arm.

"Careful!" the witch taunted. "You have a very important decision to make. Either you agree to come with us peacefully back to the Black Caldera, or these poor innocent children take a long tumble over the side of this building. Now what will it be?"

Beatrice raised both hands in the air in surrender.

"Mom, no!" Petula cried.

But the decision was made. Beatrice dropped her perfumier bottle and it rolled past Petula's feet, disappearing over the side of the hotel. An instant later, she was snared in a crackling net of electricity. She didn't fight or struggle; she simply gazed at Petula

with a soft expression that said, "Everything will be all right."

Petula watched helplessly as a witch slung Beatrice over her broom like a sack of grain before hopping on beside her. "Come on, girls," she said. "Let's deliver our prize to the queen."

"But what about the hotel?" another witch asked. "Calvina wants that, too!"

"One thing at a time! I bet the queen won't even care about the stupid hotel once she has Beatrice the Bold in her grasp!"

Worrin lunged toward the witches. "You won't get away with this," he snarled in a much nastier voice than Petula had ever heard.

But the witches ignored him, jumping onto their brooms and soaring into the sky. Petula stared helplessly after her mother, shrinking smaller and smaller as she and her captors faded into the distant Malwoods.

Petula slumped to the ground. "This is all my fault. I should have listened to my mother. I should never have interfered!"

"Oh, but what a story!" Mr. Vanderbelly exclaimed, creeping out from behind the chimney. His pen was a blur as he scribbled onto his notepad:

"BRAVE DAUGHTER ATTEMPTS TO SAVE MOTHER, BUT FAILS SPECTACULARLY!"

Worrin patted Petula on the shoulder. "You tried your best. I only wish I could have helped."

Petula groaned in dismay. But then a croak caught her attention, and she turned to see one of the crows peeping out of the birdhouse.

"You saved my bottle! Oh thank you!" she said, taking it from the bird's beak. "It's my only one. Not that it does any good when I drop it in the middle of a fight."

"Don't blame yourself," Worrin said. "We'll get Beatrice back. I'll set a course for the Malwoods right now."

"No," Petula said. "We can't drag everyone into danger. Mom wouldn't want us to."

But Worrin shook his head. "There is no discussion. Beatrice is part of the family, and we're going to get her back. We're sending this hotel into the

Black Caldera!"

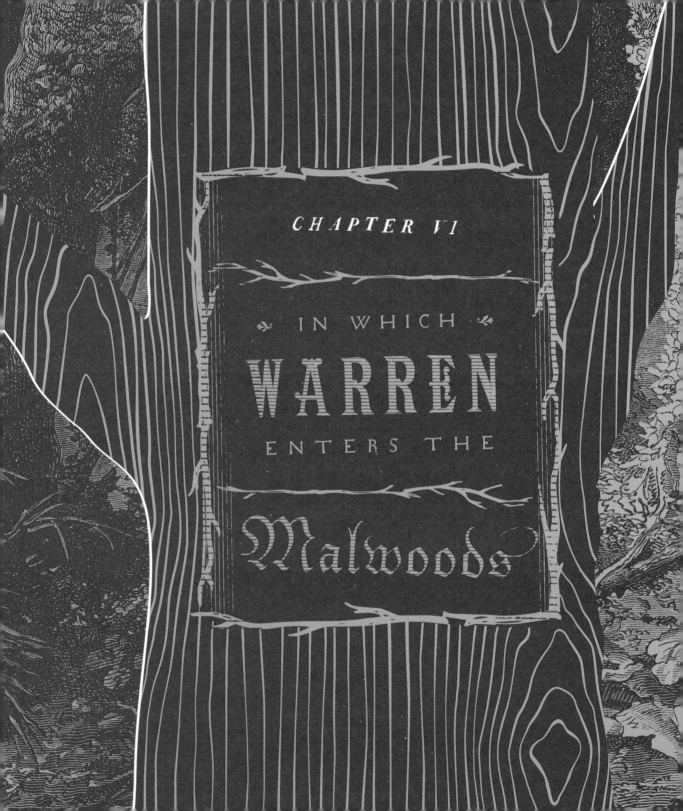

# CHAPTER VI

### ❧ IN WHICH ❧

# WÄRREN

## ENTERS THE

# Malwoods

 s soon as Warren stepped into the forest, the air seemed to turn moist and humid. The surrounding gloom felt like a thick and heavy cloak. It was such a startling contrast to the sunny, open plains he had just been walking across—as if he'd stepped into another world, one where sunlight didn't exist.

Warren hesitated as the gravity of the situation fell upon him. He was just a twelve-year-old boy entering one of the scariest territories on earth. Was he crazy to think

he'd ever catch the hotel?

*I have to try,* he told himself. His friends and family were in danger—not to mention his beloved hotel. For twelve generations, his ancestors had cared for and preserved the old building. Warren couldn't let a shape-shifter deliver it into the hands of witches and their evil queen.

Warren quickened his pace, walking with renewed determination.

But he had to be careful. There was no clear path through the forest, and along the ground, roots and vines wrestled for space. Warren tripped or stumbled every time he dared to look around. Every now and then

he'd hear the snap of a twig, and he'd turn to discover a harmless forest creature: a deer, a frog, a chipmunk. Upon closer inspection, however, Warren realized these were not ordinary animals. The deer had three eyes. The frog had pointy teeth. The chipmunk had two heads. They didn't seem to mean him any harm; they simply watched from a distance. But just to be safe, Warren grabbed a sturdy branch to use as a walking stick.

The trek reminded him of his dear labyrinth back at the original site of the Warren Hotel. When Warren used to play there, he would imagine himself as JACQUES RUSTYBOOTS, the main character from his favorite pirate adventure books, and he would pretend that the hedge maze was a wild jungle filled with surprises and peril.

But those were just idle games; this was real life. He truly was in a wild jungle [well, a wild forest, anyway], and the threats were not imagined. This both thrilled and terrified Warren as he thwacked at bushes and low-hanging branches. He felt brave and ferocious, eager to reach the hotel so he could confront the mimic and take back his birthright.

Warren even felt bold enough to sing a Jacques Rustyboots song:

# THE BALLAD OF
# JACQUES RUSTYBOOTS

Accordion

Vocal Melody

Oh ho ho! Jacques Ru-sty-boots be my name! And

Trav'- ling the globe be my claim to fame! No mon-ster of land, nor air,

nor sea Will ev-er suc- ceed in frigh-t'n- ing me! For I be cle-ver

Warren sang it several times, feeling quite cheerful indeed. But soon he noticed that the forest around him was growing darker. The sun was setting and he stopped singing, realizing that dusk might not be the best time to call attention to himself.

The long walk was also taking a toll. His short legs were growing tired and his shoulders were beginning to ache. Warren felt he was making good progress and stopped to consult his map. The good news was that he was on the right track. The bad news was that, after a full afternoon of walking, he wasn't even halfway to the Black Caldera. And the worst news was that he was traveling in a narrow channel between two witch villages, Bog Villa and Festering Ferns. As long as he continued in a northeasterly direction, he seemed likely to avoid trouble. But to do so, he'd have to pay close attention to his compass and not veer off track.

As he tucked his map into his backpack, Warren saw the food and remembered he was hungry. In his rush to catch the hotel, he still hadn't eaten anything! So he pulled out a Sap-Mallow Surprise and peeled open the foil wrapper, his mouth watering in anticipation. The chocolate had melted a bit, but the spongy marshmallow had held up nicely, and Warren chewed the candy in bliss. He was tempted to eat the whole thing, but he set aside the last bite for Sketchy.

*I wish Sketchy were here now,* Warren thought sadly. Jacques Rustyboots always had his trusty pet macaw McCrackers at his side, as well as a host of other brave friends. Warren was all alone, and night was quickly approaching. Yet as worried as he was for his own safety, he was even more concerned for his friends back at the hotel. He imagined the mimic wreaking havoc, and he hoped that somebody would realize the shapeshifter was not really him. But what if they didn't? What awful things was the impostor doing in his name? Warren gritted his teeth with renewed determination and shoved to his feet. He had to keep going.

Warren picked up his pace but only stumbled more as night settled around him. The air grew chill and a thick fog rolled in,

blanketing the forest floor with undulating waves of mist, making it harder to see obstacles in his path.

The nocturnal woodland creatures began to stir in a symphony of chittering, rustling, and croaking. In the distance, owls *HOO HOO*-ed with their hollow voices, and all around leaves were crunching from movements unknown. A bat burst out of a shrub, causing Warren to cry out. The bat flapped off into the night, screeching, but its cries were cut short as a hawk swooped out of the trees and swallowed it whole.

Soon it was almost impossible to see anything, so Warren fumbled for a lantern he'd strapped to his pack. Its glimmer did little to penetrate the murk, casting eerie shadows all around. That's when the whispering started.

It was subtle at first, a creepy chorus of sibilant noise, and seemed to be coming from all directions.

Warren dove into a bush and blew out his lantern, certain that witches were lurking nearby. He peeped out between the leaves, half out of fright, half out of curiosity. He saw nothing, but the whispering grew louder and clearer. The sounds were molding together now, and Warren could make out words but still didn't understand

them. Whatever the whispers were saying, it seemed to be in a different language.

Warren waited uneasily, expecting a procession of witches to appear, but none ever did. The whispering continued to grow louder and more urgent, repeating the chant again and again; the hairs on the back of Warren's neck stood on end. *Were they ghosts?* he wondered. His eyes had adjusted to the darkness, but all he could see were the tall pines rustling in the breeze.

After some time, the whispering grew softer and softer until it died away, leaving Warren to wonder if he'd heard it at all. He crawled out of his hiding place but realized it was too late to proceed much farther. *I need to rest and regain my strength,* he thought glumly and looked about for a place to sleep.

A hollow log seemed promising, until Warren poked into the opening and three golden eyes glowed back at him. "Sorry! I'm sorry!" he said, backing away.

Next, he peeked under a wide bush, but a large tarantula was crouched there and hissed when he approached. "Whoops, I beg your pardon!" Warren said hastily.

Finally, he spotted a cozy-looking oak tree with a ring of fallen leaves around its trunk. Warren patted them into a makeshift bed. "I guess this place is as good as any," he said. At least no other critters had claimed the spot for themselves.

Warren used his knapsack as a pillow and covered himself with leaves. They were a bit itchy, but at least he felt camouflaged. Overcome with exhaustion, he slipped almost instantly into a deep, dreamless sleep.

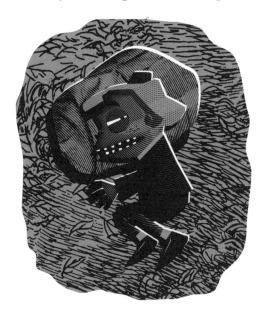

The next morning, Warren awoke to the sound of snuffling. Blearily, he opened his eyes. It was well past dawn and the sun was high in the sky, but the forest was still drenched in a dreary gray pallor. Only a few thin beams of light were tenacious enough to break through the foliage overhead.

Warren sat up and peered around, blinking his eyes into focus. When he saw the source of the snuffling, he almost jumped out of his skin. Not thirty feet away, an enormous shaggy creature was walking about on two legs and grasping at pine trees. A sap-squatch! The creature carried itself like an ape but had a face like a bear, minus the snout but with two rows of sharp teeth. Its white fur was matted with dirt and twigs. Warren glanced around in panic, desperate for a place to hide. There were no rocks or shrubs large enough to

shield him. He was still partially covered with leaves from the night before, but what if the sap-squatch found him by scent or stepped on him by accident?

THERE WAS ANOTHER LOUD *SNUFF* as the sap-squatch ambled closer. He grasped a pine tree and shook it hard, then growled in frustration. Warren couldn't help but notice that the sap-squatch seemed interested only in the pine trees, not the spindly birches or twisted junipers growing nearby.

Warren glanced up at the oak that towered over his sleeping spot. Unlike the squat pines that populated most of the forest, the oak was tall, with wide branches that looked easy to climb. Quietly shrugging his knapsack onto his shoulders, Warren grasped one of the lower branches and hoisted himself up. He felt a shudder and paused. Was it an earthquake? Or had he imagined it? He glanced down again at the sap-squatch, snarling as it grasped another pine trunk and raked the bark.

Warren scrambled up to the next tier of branches. He felt another shudder, even more violent than the first. Warren almost lost his grip as leaves rained down around him.

What was happening?

The sap-squatch was even closer now, and it seemed increasingly agitated. Warren knew he wasn't high enough to escape notice. He'd have to climb more if he hoped to hide successfully.

But when he scrambled up to the next branch, the tree shook so hard that Warren realized it was trying to throw him off. "Oh no!" Warren gasped as he clung to the trunk. "Please, let me up!"

To his astonishment, a face materialized out of the trunk; it bore the weathered appearance of a grouchy old man. "Pesky boy!" grumbled the tree. "Why don't you leave me alone! I didn't become a tree so people would climb all over me!"

The tree's statement was odd, but Warren didn't have time to ponder its meaning. "Shhh," he whispered. "There's a sap-squatch down there!"

"So?" the tree replied sourly. "Sap-squatches are everywhere." He paused thoughtfully. "Well, they used to be, anyway. That's the first one I've seen in some time."

"I'm afraid it's going to eat me," Warren said.

"Well, that's your problem!" the tree said with another toss of its branches. "Now get off of me!"

"Please!" Warren cried.

Meanwhile, the sap-squatch was getting closer and closer. It stopped walking and cocked an ear, as if hearing Warren's voice on the wind. Warren held his breath and remained still until the creature shook its head and resumed snuffling.

"Please," Warren repeated, this time in a whisper. "I'll offer you something in return!"

"What could an ugly boy like you have to offer me?" The tree's branches shook with laughter. "Years ago, I may have asked for money or fame. I wasn't always a tree, you know. But I grew tired of being a nobody, always pretending to be something I wasn't. I'm so glad I'm not nobody anymore!"

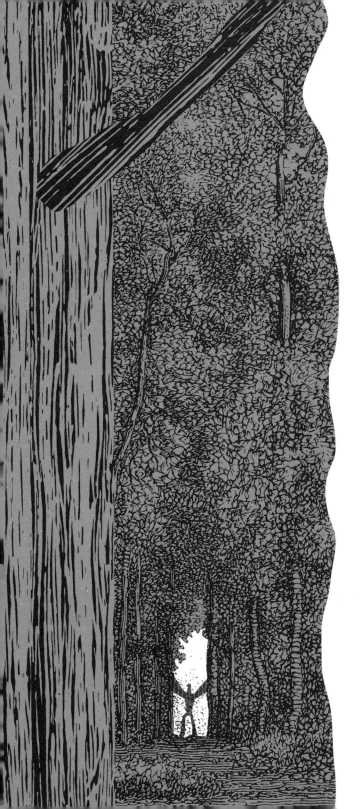

"I bet it's very nice to be a tree," Warren said.

The tree seemed pleased by this response. "Well, then, at least you have common sense. But let's see if you have the smarts to back them up. If you can solve my riddle, I'll let you hide in my branches."

"Of course!" Warren said with relief. He was quite proud of his riddle-solving abilities.

"What do a tooth, a tree, and a king all have in common?" rumbled the tree.

Warren chewed his lip. He didn't know the answer off the top of his head. He glanced back at the sap-squatch, which had abandoned the log and was now lumbering in Warren's direction. Warren hoped he could solve the riddle quickly because he didn't have much time to spare.

A king and a tree have arms, Warren thought. But a tooth doesn't.

The sap-squatch shook another pine and growled.

A king and a tooth have a mouth, but a tree doesn't . . .

The sap-squatch growled again. He was getting angrier.

An idea formed in Warren's mind. "I've got it!" he said. "Is it a cavity?"

The tree shook its branches violently. "No!"

Warren lost his grip and slipped to a lower branch. It took nearly all of his strength, but he managed to hold on. "But that was a clever guess," the tree admitted. "So I'll give you one more chance!"

Sweat broke out on Warren's brow. He'd been so sure his guess was correct. What else could it be?

Suddenly the sap-squatch looked up and its beady black eyes fixed onto Warren. Then it bared its teeth and let out a mighty roar.

"A crown!" Warren exclaimed. A king wears a crown on his head. The top of a tooth is called a crown. And the leaves and branches growing out of a tree trunk are known as a crown. "That's what they all share! A crown!"

The tree stopped shaking. "That is correct!"

Warren wasted no time. He grasped the branch above him and scurried up just as the sap-squatch charged toward the oak tree, colliding with the trunk in a mighty crash. The tree shook so hard that Warren nearly lost his grip, but he continued onward and upward, nimble as a cat, thanks to years of climbing gutter pipes and winding stairways in the hotel.

The sap-squatch's roars grew fainter as the thick leaves of the oak tree smothered the sounds below. Warren paused to catch his breath and sighed with relief.

"Thank you, Mr. Tree," he said. But the tree's scowling face had melded back into the bark, and there was no response.

 ueen Calvina stared down at Beatrice the perfumier, now bound and shackled to a pillar in a palace cell. With her wrists tied, Beatrice's magic was neutralized; she would be unable to conjure even the smallest of spells.

Calvina was wearing her most fearsome battle mask, made from the skull of an extinct manticore. Usually her victims were terrified by the sight, but Beatrice didn't seem frightened at all. She stared back at Calvina with a cold, hard expression.

"At last," the queen said aloud. "The famous Beatrice the Bold is in my grasp. My girls say you barely put up a fight! Could it be that you're losing your edge?"

Beatrice said nothing.

Calvina's coven hovered nearby, buzzing with excitement.

"Your Royal Darkness, what about our reward?" asked the blue-haired witch.

"Not now!" Calvina roared. "I'm busy with an interrogation!"

The queen turned back to her captive and smiled sweetly from behind the mask. "You understand why we might be a tad upset with you, yes? You've captured quite a few of our sisters over the years."

"Including two just yesterday," said a witch with rotten teeth. "She vanquished Kragga and Pink!"

"Is that so?" the queen asked.

Beatrice said nothing.

Calvina reached forward and rummaged through Beatrice's pockets. With a triumphant glare, she pulled out two tiny perfume bottles, each filled with a swirling, cloudy substance. "Why, here they are!"

The queen dashed the bottles to the floor, shattering the glass into thousands of pieces.

The smell of rotten eggs filled the air, and from putrid purple smoke emerged the two captured witches, looking slightly worse for wear.

"Kragga! Pink!" cried the coven sisters, ecstatic with joy.

The latter, with her brittle pink hair, spun around and snarled at Beatrice. "YOU! You'll pay for this! Do you have any idea what it's like being trapped in one of those cursed bottles?!"

Beatrice said nothing.

The Queen removed her mask and approached Beatrice.

"We'll have our revenge soon enough," the queen said. "First, we need to gather a bit of information." She turned to Beatrice, placing a hand beneath the perfumier's chin. "Be a dear and tell us where the rest of your bottles are. If you cooperate, we won't have to hurt you. Not as badly, anyway."

Beatrice said nothing.

The queen grew angry. "Why don't you speak? Say something!"

Still Beatrice didn't speak—she couldn't, of course. She simply stared back at the queen through hard mahogany eyes.

"The hotel!" Calvina exclaimed, whirling to face her coven. "The bottles must be in the hotel! What have you done with it?"

The witches exchanged uneasy glances. "We thought the perfumier would be enough to make you happy," Kragga said.

"My notice was crystal clear!" the queen cried. "I wanted Beatrice the Bold and the hotel!"

"So we don't get our heart's desire?" Kragga asked bitterly.

"No, you do not!"

## "DON'T WORRY, YOUR ROYAL DARKNESS,"

Pink assured her. "The hotel is on its way here as we speak. Some mimic pretending to be an ugly toad-boy has taken control of it. No one seemed to realize he was a shape-shifter, but I saw right through his disguise!"

For the first time, Beatrice's eyes betrayed a flicker of worry—which did not escape Calvina's notice. "Does that concern you? Good. Because when the hotel arrives, I'll allow you to watch as I destroy everyone inside. That is, unless you tell me where your bottles are hidden!"

Beatrice cast her eyes downward and said nothing.

"Well, then, let's go, girls," Queen Calvina ordered, leading her coven out of the cell. "Our prisoner will talk sooner or later if she knows what's good for her. Otherwise, she'll see what happens to those who refuse to cooperate. Now, where is my hand mirror?"

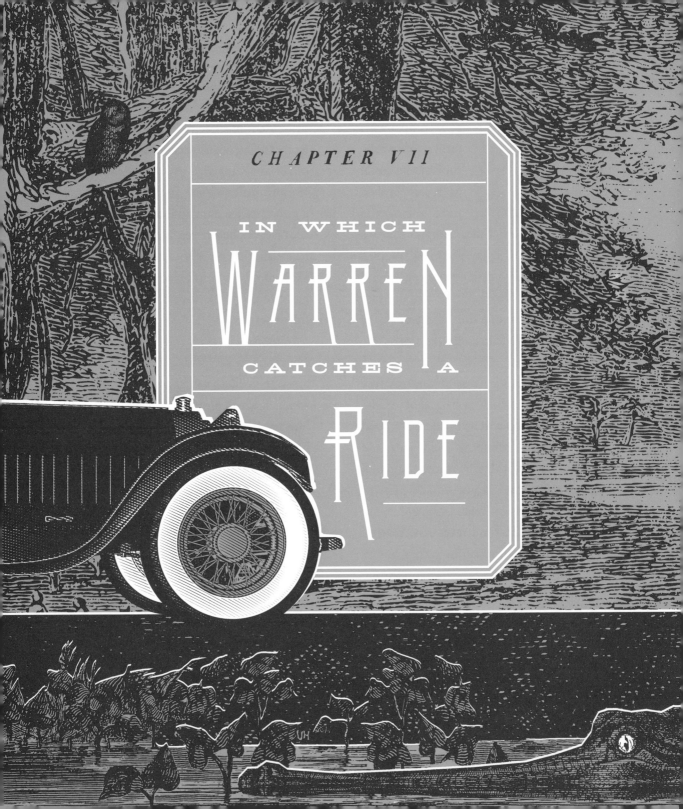

CHAPTER VII

IN WHICH

WARREN

CATCHES A

RIDE

s a very young boy, Warren used to accompany his father onto the roof of the hotel to repair broken tiles, unclog the chimney, or sometimes simply share a picnic lunch and enjoy the view. Warren loved feeling taller than everything around him. He loved pretending he was a pirate in the crow's nest of a ship. Most of all, he loved feeling as if he could see the whole world all at once.

Warren's hiding place in the oak tree wasn't nearly as high as the roof of the Warren Hotel, but it still offered a good view of the surrounding Malwoods. He stood on one of the uppermost branches, squinting into the gloomy sun. The tips of the many pine trees created a spiny blanket over the earth. To the distant east, Warren saw a silvery band, which he recognized as the ocean. He searched the horizon for the hotel, finally spotting it many miles to the north, so far away that it was barely visible. He consulted his map and confirmed that the hotel was marching steadily toward the Black Caldera. His heart fell. How would he ever catch it at this rate?

Far below, the sap-squatch had moved on to other trees, shaking them vigorously in search of precious sap. Birds tossed from their roosts scattered into the sky, squawking angrily at the disturbance. Warren waited until the sap-squatch was a safe distance away before climbing down the tree. But before reaching the ground, he heard another set of footsteps approaching. He glanced down and saw two witches trampling through the forest, carrying baskets full of berries.

One was so frail and thin, she looked like a walking twig wearing rags. Her stringy brown hair hung to her ankles, which were wrapped with colorful beads and seashells. Her teeth were filed into sharp points, and her eyes were solid black, giving her the menacing look of a shark. Her companion was short and stout, with green eyes and an elaborate hairdo that made her appear twice as tall. Bones and sticks adorned her voluminous coiffure, along with a mouse or two. Warren could overhear their conversation as they passed.

1.

"Have you heard about Beatrice the Perfumier?" asked the twiggy witch.

Warren's ears perked up.

"What's that?" asked the hairdo witch.

"Queen Calvina's coven has captured her! She's being held at the royal palace!"

Warren stifled a gasp.

"Is that so?" hairdo witch asked. "Well, perhaps all the witches Beatrice has trapped over the years will now be freed!"

"We can only hope," twiggy witch said with a nod. "She captured one of my second cousins, twice removed, so for me it's personal!"

Warren's stomach twisted with anxiety. Beatrice was one of the best witch hunters of all time. If she had been captured, what did that mean for the rest of his friends?

Before the witches could continue their conversation, they were distracted by a chugging automobile engine. It was the customer from the Sundry Shoppe! He was driving along on a nearby road, and the witches walked out of the forest to meet him.

The man stopped and then exited his car, bowing with a dramatic flourish. "Good morning, ladies! How are you this fine day?"

"Who are you?" snapped twiggy witch. "And what are you doing on our territory?"

"I mean no harm!" the man said, smiling sweetly. Warren could see his three gold teeth sparkling in the sunlight. "I was just passing through and thought you might be interested in seeing my wares!"

"Well, you thought wrong," snapped hairdo witch. "You have three seconds to get out of here or we'll make sure you never leave."

"Now, now!" the man said, holding out his hands. "No need for hostility! As a matter of fact, one of my most popular products is a calming oil. One dab and you'll feel as relaxed as a cat in the sun. It smells lovely, too. Why don't I just show you——"

"We're not interested," snarled twiggy witch. Warren held his breath as the pair advanced menacingly. The man stepped backward. "All right, all right, I get the picture. But just so you know, the witches over in Spider Cranny were much more welcoming!"

2.

"That's it!" hairdo witch cried, and then she used her fingers to shoot a sharp dagger of light at the man. He dodged sideways and the blast hit his front tire, causing it to explode with a loud *pop*.

"Look what you did!" he cried as the witches cackled. "I don't have a spare! Now I'm stranded!"

"You should've thought of that before you pestered us!" twiggy witch said. "You're lucky that tire is the only thing we deflated."

"Next time we'll pop your head!" hairdo witch added.

Still chortling, the witches picked up their baskets and strolled off as the man kicked his car in frustration.

Warren hopped out of the tree, landing in front of the man and causing him to yelp with surprise.

"You again?" he asked.

"Maybe I can help," Warren said. "I packed some heavy-duty tape in my backpack. We could use it to fix your tire."

The man looked at Warren and furrowed his brow in suspicion. "Who are you, anyway? Where are your parents?"

"I'm Warren the 13th," Warren said. "And my parents are gone. It's just me and my traveling hotel."

"Your traveling hotel?" The man's eyebrows lifted. They reminded Warren of little worms.

Warren's chest puffed out with pride. "Yes, indeed! I'm the manager and owner of the Warren Hotel! 'Where every stay is a go.'" He paused. "Well, I'm still working on the catchphrase."

"My name's Sylvester," the man said, "but you can call me Sly."

"Nice to meet you, Sly," Warren said, shaking his hand. "Now let's see if we can fix your tire."

Warren dug out his roll of tape, and Sly set about sealing up the gash. "Hey," he said, "this just may work! I have an air pump in my trunk. Mind grabbing it for me?"

Warren hurried to open the trunk. But

instead of an air pump, all he saw were wooden crates. Warren opened the nearest one and let out a yelp. Inside was a pile of snakes writhing on a nest of straw. He slammed the lid shut and moved it aside.

"Anything wrong back there?" Sly asked.

"Nothing," Warren called back, and he turned his attention to the next crate. Something large hissed from within, and a large eye blinked between the slats. An enormous white python was coiled inside, as thick as a tree trunk. Its forked tongue flitted out, tickling Warren's face. Warren realized that all the crates were full of slithering, squirming snakes.

*What kind of car is this?* he wondered. *Who drives around with a trunk full of snakes?*

Finally, he found the air pump, buried way at the bottom. He brought it around to Sly, who had finished patching the tire. "I couldn't help but notice your, uh, snakes."

"You mean my business associates," Sly said. "I'm in the snake-oil business. But here we are—look at this tire, good as new!" He handed the roll of tape to Warren. "Thanks, kid. Now we're even."

"Even?"

"Well, I unbuckled you from that chair, remember?"

"But I paid you to do that. Now you owe me a favor."

Sly grinned. "You're a canny kid, you know that? C'mere, I think I have something you'll find useful."

Sly reached into the driver's-side window and pulled out a blue leather case. He set it on the hood of the car, clicked open the latches, and lifted the lid. Inside were a dozen small bottles, all strapped into a row. Each appeared to contain some kind of amber liquid; some were as dark as molasses, others as light as honey. They reminded Warren of Beatrice's perfumier bottles.

"See here?" Sly said, pulling out a bottle from the bunch. "This'll cure a broken heart. Do you have a special someone who's left you in the dust?"

*My hotel,* Warren thought sadly. But he knew this was not the sort of answer Mr. Snake-Oil was looking for, so he shook his head.

"All right, all right, I can see you've got a resilient heart. But we're friends, right? Let me be honest with you . . ."

Sly brandished another golden bottle. "Skin problems! This will clear it right up, make you look fresh as a daisy! Whattaya say?"

"Um," Warren said, touching his face.

"Only three hundred florins. A real steal, if you ask me."

"Well...," Warren said.

"I can see you're a tough sell. You're smart, and I like that. I surely do. But tell me, you ever come across that spot you just can't clean? That stubborn grease, that dirty scuff?"

"Yes!" Warren exclaimed. If there was any subject he liked, it was cleaning.

"Well, this here oil will mop that right up! Leave a polished shine in place of any grime. And because we're pals, I'll cut you

a deal. Two hundred fifty florins. And if you buy one, I'll throw a second one in for half price. You're not gonna find a deal that good anywhere else."

"But—"

"Okay, okay. You're twisting my arm. I'll toss in a free bottle of magic hair-grow tincture. I see you got some luscious locks there, and now you can have even more! It'll flow like a golden river, like a unicorn's mane, I guarantee it!"

As the man continued to haggle, Warren sensed an opportunity. "It's really tempting," he said, "but I don't carry that kind of money around with me. I'd have to borrow it from the hotel."

"Then get in the car and let's go!" Sly exclaimed. "How far away is this hotel, anyway?"

"Not very far," Warren assured him. "If we hurry, I'm sure we can catch up soon."

"All right, then," Sly said, his golden teeth gleaming. "Hop in, kid. We've got a hotel to cash! I mean, catch!"

The jalopy's headlights cast twin beams across the road, cutting through the smothering blackness that pressed in around

them. They had been driving all day and now the jostling of the car was making Warren sleepy. Sly was humming a tune, an eerie melody that Warren didn't recognize, and his long fingers tapped on the steering wheel.

Warren glanced around at what little he could see of their surroundings. Trees and shrubs whizzed by on either side, formless shadows punctuated by the glowing eyes of watchful nighttime critters.

"Listen, kid, it's time to stop and make camp," Sly said.

"But we're getting so close!" Warren protested. In reality, he wasn't sure that was true. He still couldn't hear the hotel, which meant that it was probably a long way away. He certainly didn't want to stop now and risk falling farther behind.

"I don't want to drive all night. I need my beauty rest and my babies would appreciate a little peace and quiet, too."

"Babies?" Warren asked.

"My business associates," Sly corrected. "The snakes and I are very close."

Before Warren could beg again, Sly turned off the road and into a thick cover of trees. The jalopy jounced over the rough terrain of fallen branches and bumpy stones, setting Warren's teeth to rattling.

Sly soon found a sizable clearing to park in and yanked on the brake. The car shuddered to a stop, and he hopped out to unload the crates.

Warren also stepped out of the car and looked around in awe. Now that the engine was silent, he could hear the whispering chants once again.

"Warren!" Sly yelled from the back of the car. "Get a fire started, will ya? Those whispering voices give me the willies! They tend to shut up if there's bright light nearby."

Warren hurried to collect kindling and made a neat little pile of twigs and leaves. He was glad for the task—it reminded him of tending the many fireplaces at the hotel. He missed poking the coals and sweeping the soot; he even missed cleaning out the chimney. In fact, he missed all his chores.

As the flames snapped to life, Warren noticed that the whispers closest to them did indeed fall quiet, although he could still hear distant chants beyond the firelight.

He found a broken pine branch, still furred with needles, and used it to sweep the area clean. Sly unrolled his sleeping bag and shot Warren a curious look.

"Just tidying up," Warren explained cheerfully. "My dad used to say that you shouldn't go to bed in a messy room or else you'll have bad dreams."

"Bad dreams?" Sly said. "If that's your problem, you just need a few doses of my Sleep Magic Tonic! The good news is, I'm holding a sale on it right now! Twenty percent off per case!"

"Um, I dunno . . ."

"I'll just add it to the tab. Whattaya say?"

"Let me think about it," Warren said.

"You got anything good to eat in that pack of yours?" Sly asked. "I've been chewing on dried jerky for weeks and could use a little variety."

Warren dug through his bag and pulled out a can of beans.

Sly rubbed his hands in satisfaction. "That'll do," he said.

As he cooked the beans in a pot over the fire, Warren added a few drops from his sap jar to make them taste even better.

"Where'd you get that bottle?" Sly asked sharply. "Pure sap is hard to come by these days."

"It was the last one at the Sundry Shoppe."

"How much you want for it?"

Warren placed a hand protectively over his jacket pocket, where the bottle lay. "Sorry, but it's not for sale. I'm saving it for a friend."

"I guess it doesn't matter," Sly grunted. "Once I'm rich, I can buy all the sap I want."

After lumbering off to the car to feed his snakes a meal of dried crickets, Sly returned with several "babies" wrapped around his arms and neck. Warren cringed but said nothing. For dessert, he and Sly split a sappy candy bar and fell into an easy silence as the fire snapped and crackled.

"What do you know about the whispers?" Warren asked.

"Some say it's the trees." Sly said, gently petting one of his reptilian companions.

"What are they saying?"

"Who knows, kid. It's all in some ancient language that no one understands. And frankly, I don't care to know."

"But what if it's important?"

Sly wiggled into his sleeping bag, snakes and all, and yawned loudly. "Look, kid, it's time to get some shut-eye. G'night."

Warren lay down and watched the flames leap from the fire pit. Sly might not want to know what the whispering voices were saying, but Warren sure did. The trees were obviously communicating something—but was anybody listening?

# CHAPTER VIII

# IN WHICH PETULA DISCOVERS *the* TRUTH

hat night, Petula couldn't sleep. Every time she started to drift off, she'd remember that her mother had been captured and then she'd be wide awake worrying again. Petula told herself that nothing could be done—she'd have to wait until the hotel reached the Black Caldera before taking action—but that didn't make sleeping any easier.

As soon as the sun rose, Petula went straight to her chores, grateful for the distraction. She arrived in the kitchen and found Chef Bunion cooking an elaborate breakfast of cinnamon-pecan pancakes. He didn't seem to notice that all of the guests were gone; he simply cooked for the sheer pleasure of cooking.

"I'll take two plates, please," Petula said. "I'm bringing one to Sketchy and one to Mr. Friggs."

"Coming right up!" Chef said, flipping three pancakes out of his frying pan. They landed in a tall stack on a nearby plate.

While waiting, Petula looked out the window. It was late morning and the gloom of the Malwoods was smothering. Spindly pine trees pressed in on both sides of the road, scraping the hotel with a horrible rasping. Every so often, Petula spotted a witch flying past on a broom, but so far none had been bold enough to attack. Yet she knew one would be coming soon, and she had no idea how to prepare. Protecting the hotel had always been her mother's job.

"Here you go!" Chef Bunion handed Petula two plates piled with steaming pancakes and bacon, each topped with a pat of melted butter and a vanilla bean. "Let me know how Sketchy is holding up. I miss having help around the kitchen."

"Will do," Petula said as she loaded the plates onto a cart. She rolled it out of the kitchen and down the hall toward the utility closet.

As she walked, Worrin emerged from the control room and hurried to her side. "Where are you going?" he asked.

"I'm bringing breakfast to Sketchy and Mr. Friggs."

He blocked the cart with his body. "Sketchy has already eaten."

"Well, I'd still like to visit," Petula said, attempting to push the cart forward.

Worrin pushed back harder. "The beast is highly contagious."

Was Petula imagining things, or had she noticed a strange flicker in his eyes?

"It's safer if you stay up here," Worrin continued.

"Thanks for your concern," Petula said firmly, "but I'm willing to take my chances."

And she shoved the cart forward, edging Worrin aside.

Worrin placed a hand on her arm. "It's best if we let the creature rest."

Petula hesitated. She knew how important rest was when fighting illness. And Worrin cared about Sketchy very much—maybe he was just trying to do what was best.

"Besides," Worrin added, pointing to the trays, "you should probably bring Mr. Friggs his breakfast before it gets cold."

Petula thought it was odd that Warren didn't offer to bring the food himself.

He always took pride in delivering his mentor's meals, but at dinner the evening before he had completely forgotten. Perhaps he just had a lot on his mind. After all, they were deep in one of the most treacherous forests on earth, and Warren was spending most of his time in the control room, watching the road for threats and sneak attacks.

"Very well," Petula said, "I'll visit Sketchy later."

With a wave of her arm, she drew a portal to the fourth floor and pushed the cart through. On the other side of the vortex, she wheeled it down the hall to the library and rapped on the thick wooden door.

"Come in," said Mr. Friggs.

The room smelled familiar and comfortable, a scent of ink and aged paper that made Petula want to curl up with a book and lose herself in a story. Dripping candles flickered from nearly every shelf, casting a cozy warmth across the room's cluttered contents: dusty tomes, rolls of paper, and an interesting assortment of items that Mr. Friggs had collected in his younger days as an adventurer: carved stone statues, decorative pots, chests of rusted weapons, and old coins.

On one wall hung a large map of

Fauntleroy, with pins marking every location the hotel had visited. The navigator's desk was as disorderly as the rest of the room. A sextant, a cartography compass, and an assortment of rulers and pens littered the surface, lying atop sheets of papers scribbled with equations and coordinates.

Petula nudged aside some of the mess to set down the tray.

"Mr. Friggs?" she said.

The old man's voice echoed from across the room. "Yes, dear?"

Petula navigated her way around tottering stacks of hand-bound books, following the sound of his voice. She found him brooding in a leather armchair in the darkest corner of the room. His face was obscured by shadows.

"There you are!" she said. "I brought you breakfast."

"I don't have much of an appetite, I'm afraid," Mr. Friggs said morosely. "I'm feeling quite uneasy."

"The Malwoods have that effect on people," Petula said.

"It's more than that," Mr. Friggs said. "To be candid, I'm a little concerned about our friend Warren. He skipped his tutoring session this morning. For the second day in a row."

"Really?" Petula said. "Well, I suppose we all have a lot on our minds right now. I'm sure things will return to normal once my mom is home safe and sound."

"I want to believe that's true," Mr. Friggs said, "but I have the nagging sense that Warren is different. Not himself, if you know what I mean. It's possible that he's distracted by all of this danger, but I feel as if it's something greater."

Petula knew exactly what he meant. "Something is definitely fishy," she admitted. "Ever since he went to that dentist, he hasn't been acting like himself."

"Dentist?" Mr. Friggs asked.

"At the Sundry Shoppe," Petula explained. "After we bought the De-Stickifier, Warren stayed behind to have his teeth cleaned."

"At a general store?" Mr. Friggs looked uneasy. "But why would a general store offer dentistry services? In the middle of nowhere?"

"I'm not really sure," Petula said. Now that she thought about it, the business did seem rather strange.

"Teeth are often used as tools for evil magic," Mr. Friggs said. "Remember the manticore tooth used by Warren's aunt Annaconda?"

Dread crept down Petula's spine. "Do you think there's evil magic at work here?"

"I'm not sure," Mr. Friggs said. "I need to do more research. Until I learn more, do not speak a word of this to Warren. If evil is present, we need to be prepared . . . and we need to be discreet."

"My lips are sealed," Petula promised.

Mr. Friggs pushed out of his armchair, hobbled over to a shelf, and began pulling down tattered volumes about dark magic.

"For now, our best course is to act as normal and pleasant as possible."

Petula nodded.

"Are you all right?" Mr. Friggs asked. "You look rather pale. Well, paler than usual. I hope you haven't caught whatever Sketchy has."

"I'm starting to wonder if Sketchy is even sick at all," Petula muttered.

Mr. Friggs licked his lips and flipped through the pages of one of his tomes. "I can't say for sure. Warren refuses to let me see Sketchy, so a proper diagnosis is impossible."

"He won't let me see Sketchy, either!" Petula exclaimed. With each passing moment, she became more convinced that something very bad was brewing. "Maybe Sketchy knows something we don't."

Mr. Friggs looked up, concerned. "You should attempt to find out. In the meantime, I'll review my books and see if I can learn something useful."

"Good plan," Petula said, waving her finger to draw a portal. "And if Warren comes to see you, cover for me!"

As she slipped through the portal, the world tilted and blurred until she arrived in the darkness of the utility closet. Sketchy whistled in alarm until Petula called, "It's just me!" Then she felt the creature's tentacles as it pulled her into a grateful hug. "Let's get some light in here."

Petula held up a finger and a warm glow appeared at the tip, illuminating the room. That's when she saw the drawings. They covered every surface: the walls, floors, even the ceiling. Crude drawings of Warren with glowing eyes and jagged teeth, all drawn with colored pencil.

# "SKETCHY!"

Petula said as she turned around to inspect the artwork. "Why in the world would you draw these things?"

Sketchy let out a tirade of whistles. Clearly the creature was trying to say something, but Petula couldn't understand. And there wasn't much time. Warren could be making his way to the utility room any minute, and if he saw the drawings, what then?

"Listen, Sketchy, I'm going to ask you some questions. I want you to tap your head for yes and wiggle your tentacles for no. Got it?"

Sketchy tapped its head: *Yes.*

"Great. Are you really sick?"

Sketchy wiggled its tentacles: *No.*

"I knew it!" Petula exclaimed. "Warren locked you away so you wouldn't be able to tell anyone what you know, didn't he?"

Sketchy tapped its head.

"So what do you know?" Petula said.

Sketchy froze, unsure how to answer.

"Sorry, I got excited," Petula said. "I'll stick to yes-or-no questions."

Her heart was pounding. What question could she ask that Sketchy would be able to answer? It was clear that Warren was up to something, but what?

"Is there evil magic at work?"

Sketchy tapped its head.

"Mr. Friggs was right!" Petula exclaimed. "Is Warren possessed by an evil spirit?"

Sketchy looked thoughtful, then wiggled its tentacles.

"No? But I'm close?" Petula asked.

Sketchy tapped its head again, then gestured to one of the illustrations. It depicted a friendly Warren standing side-by-side with a sinister evil twin.

# "A MIMIC?"

Petula asked. "Warren's been replaced by a mimic?"

Sketchy whistled shrilly.

"Oh my goodness!" Petula cried. "You knew this whole time that Warren wasn't Warren at all, he's an impostor!"

Sketchy spun her around, tapping her head as well as its own: *YES, YES, YES!*

"That means the real Warren is missing!" Petula cried in horror. "We need to tell Mr. Friggs right away!"

She turned to the door and tried to open it before remembering that it was locked. With concentration, she commanded the light at the end of her finger to grow into a sizzling flame. With a sudden spark, it leapt to the doorknob, which turned red hot and melted off.

"It worked!" she said with a mixture of pride and surprise. "I just learned that spell last week!"

Sketchy whistled in appreciation.

"Come on, Sketchy!" Petula said. "Let's sneak up to Mr. Friggs's library and tell him what's going on. Surely one of his books will be able to teach us how to defeat a mimic!"

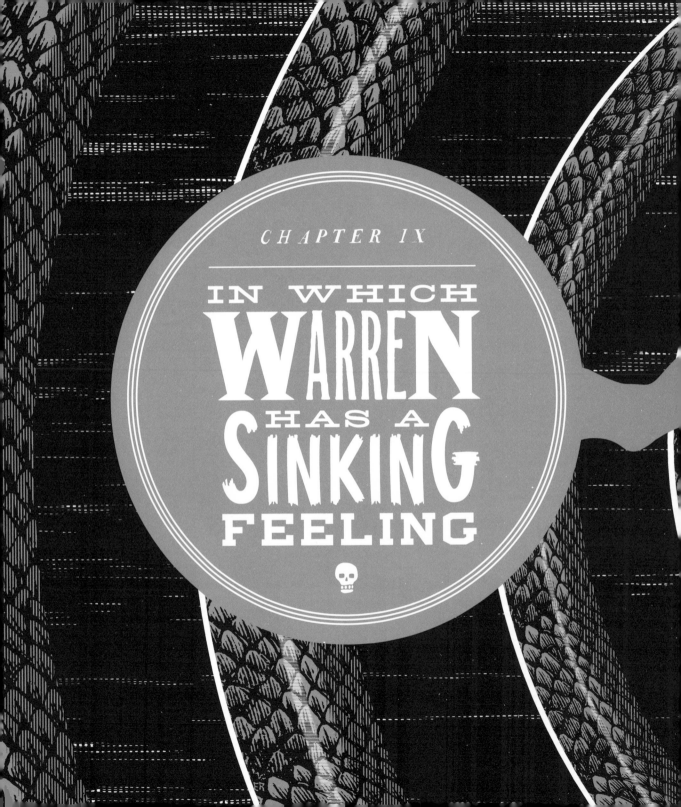

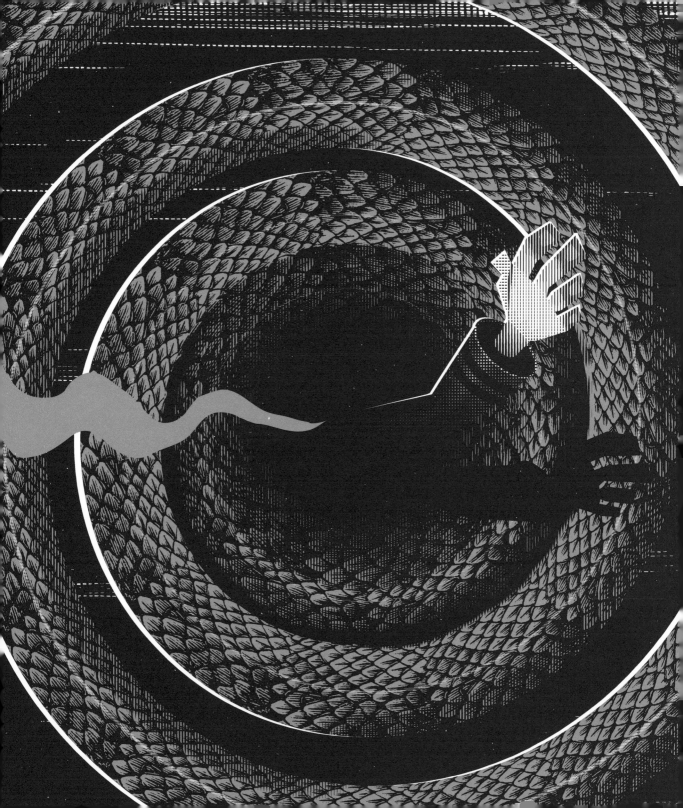

arren was in good spirits as he and Sly packed up their campsite after a breakfast of boiled peas. They loaded up the jalopy and Sly turned on the engine. "Let's catch ourselves a hotel!" he announced. "Strap in!"

Warren buckled his seatbelt as the car trundled over the terrain. When it reached the road, the ride smoothed out considerably. Sly stepped on the gas and cranked the car into high gear. They drove for several hours, bouncing along as they passed an endless groves of pine trees. Everything looked the same no matter which way you turned, so Warren was grateful for both the road and his map. There was no sun in the sky to help with navigation.

"You seem to know your way around the Malwoods," Warren said.

"I spend a lot of time here, that's for sure," Sly said. "There's a lot of opportunities for a man such as myself. The witches can't get enough of my oils. They like adding them to their brews."

"Do you ever get scared?" Warren asked.

"Oh, sure," Sly said. "I've ended up in a pickle or two, as you've seen for yourself. One time, this whole coven tried to boil me alive in a cauldron. Another time, I crossed paths with an angry sap-squatch, and I had to hide in a smelly bog to avoid it."

"I saw a sap-squatch yesterday!" Warren said.

"Is that right?" Sly asked. "I haven't seen one in a long time. Not that I'm complainin'."

Suddenly, Warren recognized a familiar sound in the distance—it was the

# CLANG-CLANG-CLANG!
## OF THE HOTEL!

"We're getting close!" he exclaimed. "I can hear it!"

"About time," Sly said. "I'm ready to sleep in a proper bed and eat a proper meal. Say, what other amenities does your hotel have? Is there a swimming pool?"

"Well, no," Warren admitted. "But we have the most comfortable rooms you'll ever stay in, and the finest meals provided by the best chef in all of Fauntleroy! We have an expansive library and a game room and a brand-new observation deck and . . ."

Warren continued regaling Sly with details about his beloved hotel while they jostled along. Warren bounced in his seat—partially from all the bumps in the road, but mostly from excitement. They were so close!

As they drove, the forest seemed to come to life. The temperature rose, and a foul-smelling fog seeped out of the ground. Strange-looking reptiles with brightly colored scales hissed and slinked through the trees, and plum-colored birds with red eyes and razor-sharp beaks shrieked from the canopy above. Everything around them seemed to crackle with a sort of dark energy that gave Warren goose bumps. It felt like the air before a thunderstorm—tingly and electric—and the faint scent of sulfur reminded him that witches were about, casting evil magic.

"Sure is something, being this deep in the forest," Sly said, looking rather pale. He stroked his long mustache nervously.

"Are you okay?" Warren asked, swatting at a fist-sized insect that whirred past his ear. He was plenty scared himself, but he didn't want to add to his companion's unease.

"Oh, I'm sure it'll all be worth it," Sly said distractedly. He seemed to be talking more to himself than to Warren.

The road got even narrower, and muddier, and Sly slowed down to avoid hitting the pine trees—trees, Warren couldn't help but notice, that were gouged with claw marks.

# SAP-SQUATCHES,

Warren thought uneasily.

The jalopy lurched. A wet squelch sounded from under the tires.

"Oh no," Warren said in dismay. "A mud puddle!"

"It's no problem," Sly said reassuringly. "This old jalopy has been through much worse. These tires are built for all kinds of tricky terrain."

But the tires didn't seem to agree. No matter how hard Sly pumped the gas pedal, they stayed stuck in place, spinning and whirring and spraying mud in all directions. Bubbles began to pop on top of the ooze.

Warren peered over the car door's edge. "Are we . . . sinking?"

Sly's eyes widened. "Dagnabbit! This ain't no mud puddle! It's . . . it's . . ."

"Quicksand!" Warren cried. He knew all about quicksand from his favorite Jacques Rustyboots books. "The more you move,

the faster you sink!"

The car gave another lurch. With a thick, slick *pop!* the front tires sank another inch, then two, then three. Sly and Warren didn't have long—the quicksand was living up to its name.

"Come on, old buddy," Sly hissed at the car, pumping the pedals. "You can do it!"

A loud *vroom* from the engine and they sank even farther. The mud had reached the headlights and was rising fast. "You're making it worse!" Warren cried. But Sly kept pumping the pedal so hard that smoke curled from under the hood.

"Come on," he said. "Come on!"

"It won't work," Warren said. "We have to abandon ship!" He looked around but didn't see a way out. They were too far from dry ground to jump to safety, and no tree branches were within reach.

"My poor jalopy!" Sly wailed. "What rotten luck!" He pounded the dashboard in desperation. Sand and mud lapped at the windshield.

"We don't have much time," Warren said. "We have to move!" The car would be filled with quicksand within a minute, maybe less.

"But what about my babies?" Sly cried. "I can't just leave them!"

Warren cringed, but he knew Sly was right. They couldn't leave the snakes to perish in the trunk. "Follow me," Warren said. "But be careful."

Delicately, Warren shimmied through the window, braced his feet on the door, and climbed onto the roof. On the other side, Sly did the same, but his weight was too much—the car started to tip toward the side.

"Help!" Sly yelled. "I'm falling!"

Warren reached over and, using all of his might, pulled Sly back onto the roof. The quicksand had swallowed almost the entire windshield and was starting to cover the side windows as well. Sly hopped to the back of the car, balancing on the bumper and throwing open the trunk.

"I need you guys to listen to me," he said, lifting the snakes one at a time. "Everything will be okay. I'm gonna toss you to shore, and I want you to slither until you've found higher ground. Save yourselves!"

And so with tears in his eyes, Sly flung the first snake across the quicksand pit and, miraculously, it landed on dry land; it

seemed dazed but unharmed and slithered off. Warren picked his way to the bumper just as Sly reached in for another crate.

"Help me out, boy! There's too many, and we don't have much time!"

As if in response, the car again heaved forward. The back was sticking up in the air like the stern of a sinking ship. Peeking into the trunk, Warren gritted his teeth. He'd hoped he'd never have to touch a snake, but he couldn't be skittish now. With eyes closed, he thrust his arms into a crate, expecting to grab something cold and slimy. But what his fingers felt was warm and dry, like pebbles in the sun. It wasn't so bad after all. With both hands full, Warren cocked

back his arms and tossed the snakes as far as he could. They arced through the air and slapped against dry land: one, two, three—but the fourth one came up short and hit the quicksand with a wet slap.

"Shirley!" Sly cried in horror.

But Shirley didn't sink. She didn't even slide. Instead, she slithered right across and wriggled onto safe ground.

"Shirley's fine!" Warren said.

Sly gasped. "Snakes can't sink!"

"But we can!" Warren said. "Hurry!" He rushed through the last of the crates, releasing the snakes to fend for themselves. Dark sand was sucking at the car doors, pulling them down faster and faster. *Think,*

Warren commanded himself, *how can we escape?* He dug into his backpack, searching for anything that might help, but the only things left were candy bars and canned food. Too much weight—he had to abandon the bag.

"Throw heavy items overboard!" Warren said, tossing his pack into the bubbling ooze. "We need to lighten our load!"

But Sly was distracted. "I nearly forgot Stella!" he exclaimed, breaking open the final crate. Warren's blood ran cold. Stella was a massive albino python. "She's a heavy girl," Sly said, grunting as he pulled the snake's front half out of the box. The serpent hissed and coiled around his shoulders, its tongue flickering as its catlike eyes gleamed. "Hurry, grab the other end!"

Quicksand was now pouring into the trunk, spilling onto the floor and oozing onto the front seats. Warren wrapped his arms around Stella's body and struggled to lift. "I can't do it!" he cried. "She's as heavy as a log!"

*Wait,* Warren thought. *Log. Bridge.* Stella was easily twenty feet long. If the other snakes hadn't sunk, then maybe . . .

"Never mind throwing Stella," Warren said, pointing to the quicksand. "Just place her on the quicksand and get ready to hitch a ride!"

"What?!" Sly cried.

"Trust me!" Warren said.

Warren and Sly eased Stella out of the car, and the snake slowly slithered across the quicksand, making her way toward dry land.

"What about my medicines?" Sly said. He clutched his chest as mud oozed over the remaining boxes, jugs, and bags piled in the carriage. "My precious oils!"

"We don't have time!" Warren said. "Come on!"

"Wait!" Sly said. "Just one thing—"

As a thin layer of mud crept over the roof, Sly lunged backward, wrapped his fingers around the blue strap of a satchel, and yanked it out of harm's way. Quicksand poured into the trunk, burying the bottles in its sticky, stinky mass. They had to go— *now*.

"Hurry!" Warren yelled. Treading carefully, he stepped off the roof and onto the python's back, yanking Sly after him. With a loud *blurp*, the rest of the jalopy disappeared.

Sly gasped, clutching his satchel.

"Don't lose your balance!" Warren warned. "Use the snake as a bridge."

Weaving and wobbling, they crept along. Stella may have been as big as a log, but she moved quite a lot; once or twice her muscles twitched so hard that Warren nearly fell off. But by carefully placing one foot in front of the other, they both made it to her scaly head and, finally, reached dry land.

Warren flopped to the ground in relief. He turned to the python, who looked balefully at him through pink eyes.

"Sorry, Stella," Warren said. "But thank you for your help. I'll never think badly of snakes again!"

Stella simply stuck out her forked tongue and said, "*Phhhhhhhhhhhbbbbt!*" before slithering away into a dense thatch of trees.

"Stella! Come back!" Sly called. He tried grabbing at the python's tail but wasn't fast enough; the snake disappeared into the trees and Sly was left holding his lone satchel in shaking hands.

"She's gone," he said, his voice hollow. "My snakes are gone. My jalopy's gone. Everything's gone. I'm ruined! Ruined, I tell you!"

"We still have our lives!" Warren said. "And all your snakes survived! You just have to start over."

"Start over?" Sly cried. "Do you have any idea how long it takes to get oil off a snake?

This is all your fault! You owe me, kid!

# YOU OWE ME BIG TIME!"

That didn't seem fair to Warren, considering that he was the one who had saved Sly's life. But all he said was, "I'm sorry. I know how hard it is to lose everything you've worked for."

"No, you don't," Sly said. "And nothing you can do will ever make up for this!" He curled his hands into fists and stood up, towering over Warren with menace in his eyes. "In fact, I oughtta—" But then he stopped midsentence, a look of horror on his face. "On second thought, never mind." To Warren's astonishment, Sly turned quickly and ran off into the woods.

"Wait!" Warren called after him. "Where are you going?"

Sly didn't dare look back. Warren glanced around to consider his location, but all he saw was a slash of white fur before everything went black.

# CHAPTER X

In Which

## PETULA

is

## SURROUNDED

etula and Sketchy crept out of the utility closet and sneaked up the stairway to the lobby. Petula tried her best to step lightly, but her shoes made a loud *click-clack* sound on the cement. Upon reaching the lobby, she and the creature tiptoed across the checkered title floor, heading toward the main stairwell.

"Why are you two sneaking around?" boomed a loud voice.

Sketchy let out a shrill whistle of alarm, wrapping its tentacles around Petula as Mr. Vanderbelly emerged from a side doorway. As usual, he was carrying his pencil and notepad.

Petula sighed with relief. "None of your business," she said.

"But I am a journalist," Vanderbelly said loftily. "Everything is my business!"

"All I'm going to tell you," Petula said, "is that you should go to your room and lock the door."

Mr. Vanderbelly looked at Sketchy and narrowed his eyes. "Isn't that creature supposed to be quarantined?"

"It's not sick," Petula said impatiently. "It never was."

"A likely story. It looks to me as if you've broken Sketchy out of quarantine! And now you're trying to move the beast to another secret location. What would Warren say if he knew about these shenanigans?"

Of course this was the last thing that Petula wanted. She knew she would have to act quickly to keep the situation from getting out of hand.

"Listen to me, Mr. Vanderbelly," she

said. "I've got an exclusive scoop for your newspaper. You can publish this information if you want, but you can't tell anyone I told you."

Mr. Vanderbelly held his pen at the ready. "Go on," he said.

"Warren isn't who you think he is. He's an impostor! A phony in disguise! And he can't be trusted! So stay out of his way, do you hear me?"

Mr. Vanderbelly snorted in disgust. "You call that a 'scoop'? That's the most ridiculous, made-up story I've ever heard! I'm going to find Warren and tell him that you're smearing his good name!"

With that, Mr. Vanderbelly spun on his heel and stomped down the stairs that led to the basement control room. Sketchy whistled menacingly.

"I know what you mean, Sketchy," Petula said, "but we can't do anything to stop him. Let's just hurry and find Mr. Friggs so we can warn him!"

They raced up the stairs and Petula flung open the doors to the library. Mr. Friggs sat surrounded by piles of books with a troubled expression on his face. "I'm afraid I'm still no closer to an answer!" he said. "I've been poring through all my books on dark magic and I haven't been able to pinpoint what has happened to Warren. It could be hypnotism, or perhaps possession by a ghost or maybe . . ."

# "A MIMIC"

Petula said, finishing his sentence.

Mr. Friggs slapped his forehead. "A mimic! But of course! How did you know?"

"Sketchy told me," Petula said. "There's no time to explain. The important thing is, do you know how to stop one?"

"Not off-hand, though I have a book somewhere. Let me see if I can find it."

Mr. Friggs stood up and began rooting through his shelves. "Is it this one? No, no . . . it was somewhere over here . . ."

"We have to hurry," Petula said.

"But I still need to do research— cross-referencing! Study!"

"Okay, then I'll do my best to buy you some time. Maybe I can lead him on a wild goose chase," Petula said. "Lock the door behind us and don't let anyone inside. Sketchy, you stay here where it's safe."

Sketchy let out a shrill whistle of protest. It was clear that it wasn't going to allow Petula to face the mimic alone.

"Oh, very well," she said. "Come on, then."

They stepped back out into the hall, and Petula could hear the *snick* of the lock being turned behind them.

"Good luck!" Mr. Friggs said through the door. "And be careful!"

Petula and Sketchy cautiously crept down the stairs. Petula held her lone perfumier bottle in her palm, ready to use it if necessary. When they reached the lobby, Petula noticed Worrin standing in the center of the checkered tile floor.

"There you are," he said. "We've been waiting for you."

"We?" Petula asked.

"Mr. Vanderbelly had some very interesting things to tell us," he continued.

"Us?" Petula asked.

"That's right," Worrin said. "Let me introduce my friends."

The light in the lobby dimmed, and the mimic's form began to separate and multiply. Surely this was some kind of dark magic; Petula reached for her perfumier bottle, taking great pains not to drop it this time. But when she uncorked it, nothing happened. Within seconds, there were thirteen copies of Worrin, surrounding Petula and Sketchy in a circle.

The Worrins laughed as if this was the funniest thing in the world. "You think that bottle will work on us?" they jeered in unison. "We're not witches! We're mimics, and our magic is immune to your perfumier weapons!"

Petula gritted her teeth in frustration. Her perfumier skills would be useless against the mimic. The duplicates closed the circle, moving in closer to Petula and Sketchy, like a knot being pulled tight.

"Stay back!" Petula warned, still holding out the useless bottle.

"Or what?" the Worrins sneered. "You can't do anything and you know it!"

Petula whirled and cast the sparkling fire spell that she had used to melt the lock in the utility room. It zapped one of the Worrins and the mimic burst into shadowy smoke,

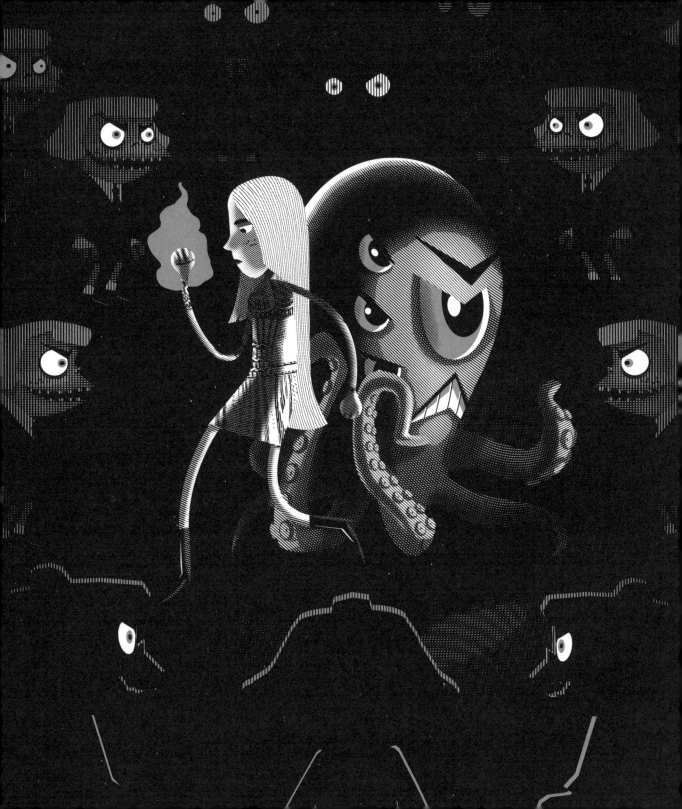

but it wasn't enough to stop the other twelve. They lunged forward, a mob of shadowy arms and hands. Sketchy whistled in anger, slapping the mimics with its tentacles.

# "PUT US DOWN!" PETULA YELLED.

But it was no use—she and Sketchy were sorely outnumbered.

"We're sorry, but you have overextended your stay," the Worrins droned.

"Chef!" Petula screamed. "Mr. Vanderbelly!"

"We're afraid they can't hear you," the Worrins continued. "Mr. Vanderbelly is interviewing Chef for a feature article, and it'll be some time before they realize you're no longer on board!"

The front doors crashed open and the Worrins pushed Petula and Sketchy out onto the porch. The road yawned before them, a good fifty feet below. The hotel's legs were so tall that a drop from the first floor would almost certainly be fatal.

Petula managed to zap another of the Worrins into smoke, but the situation was hopeless—there were too many to fend off. She let out a cry as the Worrins booted her and Sketchy out of the lobby doors and they tumbled down, down, down toward the road below. Petula closed her eyes, expecting the worst. She knew death was imminent, and in her last moments she wished her mother would find a way to escape from the witches, and somehow restore control of the hotel.

Then, all of a sudden, Sketchy's tentacles curled around Petula's waist, wrapping her in what felt like a cocoon. An instant later, they hit the ground—and then bounced back up, just like a rubber ball.

"Sketchy!" Petula cried. "Are you okay?"

The creature trilled patiently as they bounced again and again, finally rolling to a stop at the side of the road. Only then did Sketchy release Petula, using one of its tentacles to tap the side of its head: *Yes, I'm okay.* Finally it shook itself all over, like a dog shedding water.

As for the hotel, it was already walking away, but was still within range for them to reenter using one of Petula's portals. She waved her casting arm and one appeared instantly.

"Well, come on!" she said, tugging on one of Sketchy's tentacles as she stepped into the swirling pool of magic. "This will take us directly to the library!" She felt resistance as Sketchy refused to budge. "What's wrong?" she asked. "We have to hurry!"

Sketchy whistled in distress and Petula realized the problem. He was too big to fit inside her portal! She gritted her teeth and tried her best to make it larger. She hopped out and dug her heels into the dirt as she pushed on Sketchy's rubbery hide, trying to squeeze him through the opening. But it was no use: Sketchy's bulbous head was simply too large to fit.

"I can't make it any larger," Petula said. She already felt dizzy from the effort. Sketchy pointed at the hotel, which was rapidly receding in the distance. The creature chirped and whistled, nudging Petula toward the portal she had made.

"You want me to go ahead and leave you here?" Petula asked, and Sketchy tapped its head. She glanced back at the hotel—if she didn't move quickly, the hotel would be out of range and her portal wouldn't work at all. But she couldn't do it.

"I'm not going to leave you alone in this horrible place," she told Sketchy. "We'll just have to find another way to catch up to the hotel." Sketchy whistled and gave her a hug. Then it scooped Petula onto its back, and with surprising speed it hurried down the road after the hotel. With eight tentacles instead of two legs, Sketchy was able to gallop much like a horse. But despite this burst of speed, the hotel was still much faster, and within minutes it had faded out of sight.

Petula felt a wave of despair. She wasn't sure how they would ever catch up to a building that moved faster than an automobile, but she knew they had to try. *We owe it to Warren to save his hotel*, Petula thought to herself. *I just hope he's okay, wherever he is . . .*

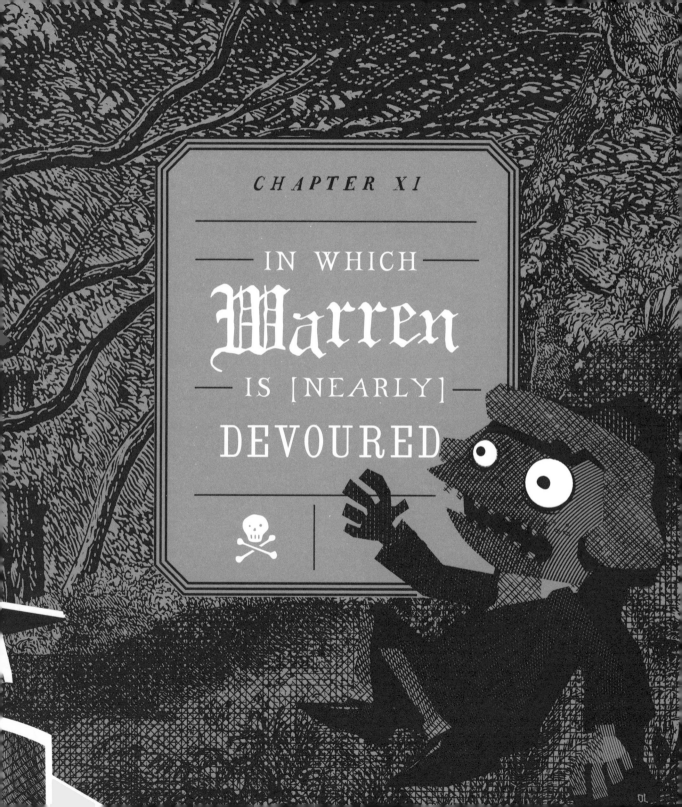

**S**tars danced before Warren's eyes as he slowly regained consciousness. Through the fog of a throbbing headache, he could smell a warm, toasty fire that reminded him of Chef Bunion's kitchens. It was the comforting smell of home.

He tried to rub his sore head but realized his hands were bound. As his vision cleared, he saw that he was wrapped tightly in vines, and that the giant sap-squatch was standing just a few feet away. The monster was crouching over a large fire, tying branches into an elaborate construction that hung just above the flames. He appeared to be building a spit for roasting meats.

"Is that . . . for me?" Warren asked.

The sap-squatch ignored the question. He continued bending and twisting branches with his massive bear-like paws. Even though Warren was cocooned in vines, he found that he could rock back and forth. So he rocked and rocked and rocked until he built enough momentum to roll his body closer to the sap-squatch.

"Hello?" he called. "Excuse me, Mr. Sap-Squatch?"

The sap-squatch glanced up but didn't reply.

"I have an idea," Warren said. "If you let me go, I'll help you find a better meal."

The sap-squatch snorted. "That seems highly unlikely," he said.

To Warren's astonishment, the creature spoke in a crisp English accent and with perfect diction.

"In fact," the sap-squatch continued, "the trees in this forest haven't produced sap in years. All of the animals are poisonous, and I would never dare eat a witch." He shrugged.

"So that leaves you, I'm afraid. I regret that it's come to this, but I haven't had a bite in days and something about you smells quite delicious."

The sap-squatch lowered his nose to Warren's jacket, sniffing furiously. Warren realized what he found so irresistible: the sap bottle in his pocket!

"I know where we can find some sap," Warren said. "If you set me free, I'll get you an entire bottle of sap within minutes!"

The sap-squatch's eyes glowed with excitement. "How do I know this isn't a trick?"

"Mr. Sap-Squatch, I am the manager of a hotel. I would never lie to my guests, and I wouldn't lie to you either. My father taught me to be honorable!"

The sap-squatch scratched his chin with a long claw, pondering his decision. After a moment, he nodded his shaggy head and said, "Well . . . I suppose that's as good an argument as any. Very well, I'll set you free. But if you deceive me, I shall eat you raw!"

With a single swipe of his claws, the sap-squatch severed the vines around Warren's limbs. Warren let out a sigh of relief, then reached into his pocket and retrieved the bottle he'd taken from the Sundry Shoppe. "And here you are," he said. "A promise is a promise."

As soon as the sap-squatch took the bottle, his mood changed instantly.

"Oh sap! Oh my sweet, sweet sap! How I've missed you!" he cried, hugging the bottle to his furry chest. He uncorked it and began guzzling the contents greedily with loud *glug-glug-glug* noises.

"Maybe you should save some for later?" Warren suggested. "So you have something to look forward to."

The sap-squatch sighed and reluctantly recorked the bottle. "You're right. It's just so hard to resist! It's been weeks and weeks since I've had a drop of sap and it's driving me mad! I feel much better now."

"Well, I'm sure glad to hear that," Warren said, laughing nervously. "Sometimes I get cranky when I'm hungry, too. My friend Chef Bunion calls it a case of the grumpy grumbles."

"That sounds accurate," the sap-squatch concurred.

"But I'm confused," Warren said. "This whole forest is full of pine trees. Have they all run out of sap?"

"That's what I've been trying to find out. I risked everything to escape the Black Caldera to try and bring sap back to my people."

"You're from the Black Caldera?" Warren asked.

"Not by choice. The queen has enslaved all the sap-squatches and feeds us sap in return for our labor, but it's never quite enough. We've become so sickly . . ." He paused to wipe away a tear. "Once sap flowed from every tree, and sap-squatches roamed the forest freely, drinking as much as we needed. Now the trees are empty. I keep hoping to find even one that still has sap, but so far no luck."

"If all the trees have stopped giving sap, where does the queen get hers?" Warren asked.

"I don't know," the sap-squatch said. "My greatest fear is that she'll run out, too, and then my people truly will die."

"How awful!" Warren cried. "She must be stopped!"

"I wish it were that easy. We sap-squatches outnumber the witches, but we've become too weak and ill to fight back."

"There must be a way," Warren said. "If we find the queen's hidden supply of sap, would that give your people enough strength to fight back?"

"It might, but I've already searched the entire crater. I haven't been able to figure out where she keeps it."

"I'll help you figure it out," Warren said. "I'm on my way to the Black Caldera now. If you help me save my friends and get my hotel back, I'll help you find the sap." Warren held out his hand. "What do you say?"

The sap-squatch's paw was so large, he simply grasped Warren's hand with a thumb and forefinger. "It's a deal!"

"I still don't know your name," Warren said.

"I beg your pardon! I've completely forgotten to introduce myself. My name is"—and the sap-squatch threw back his head and released an ear-splitting roar.

"I see," Warren said, after his ears stopped ringing. "I'm not sure I can pronounce that.

WHAT IF I JUST CALL YOU SIR SAP?"

"Ooh, I rather like that! And I shall call you Smelly, because you smell delicious."

"Well, my name is Warren the 13th," Warren said.

"Excellent, Smelly! Shall we be on our way?"

Warren sighed. At least his nickname wasn't "Lunch"!

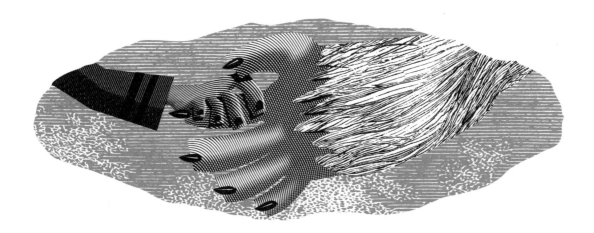

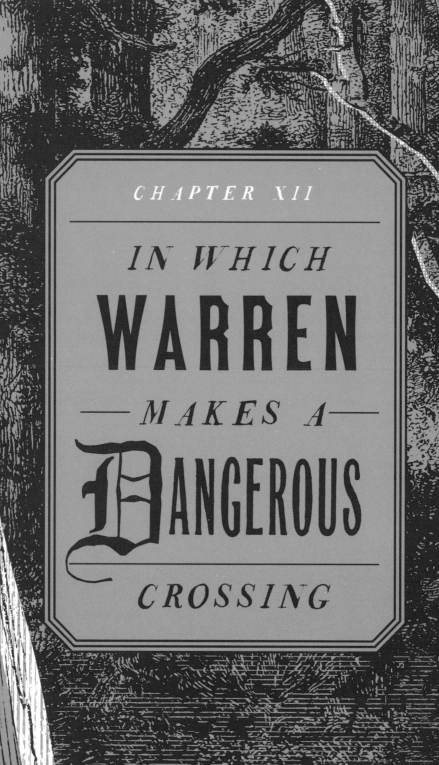

CHAPTER XII

IN WHICH

WARREN

MAKES A

DANGEROUS

CROSSING

ir Sap led the way toward the Black Caldera, with Warren following close behind. He no longer needed to consult his map. Sir Sap knew the forest like the back of his paw, and he proceeded with confidence. Warren had a hard time keeping up with the creature's long strides, but he did his best as they marched through endless groves of trees.

As they drew closer to the crater, the landscape changed. Dense forest gave way to rockier hills, some of which sparkled with waterfalls. Sir Sap showed Warren which ones were safe to drink from and which were not, and Warren was glad to have something to quench his thirst; the bottles of Sappy Cola had sunk in the quicksand, along with all of his other food and supplies.

As the day wore on, they climbed over groping roots and wound up and down steep switchbacks that made Warren's calves ache. They skirted toxic puddles bubbling with putrid orange and green liquid, and ducked through moist tunnels made from hollowed-out logs. The air grew stickier and more humid with every mile, and Warren soon began to sweat. He felt bad for Sir Sap with his shaggy coat, but the sap-squatch barely seemed to notice the heat.

"Aren't you hot under all that fur?" Warren asked him.

"Not at all!" Sir Sap said. "Sap-squatches have special coats that keep us cool in hot weather and warm in cold weather."

Warren wiped sweat from his brow. "That sounds nice," he said.

"Not only that, but our coat has special oils that keep sap from sticking to us. It just slides right off. Quite helpful when we're dining, of course."

The walk was long and uncomfortable but Sir Sap's company made the hard journey tolerable. He was easy to talk with and happy to play tour guide, sharing random tidbits about the Malwoods as they trudged along.

"Over that way is the witch village of Poxville," Sir Sap said, pointing west. "True to its name, the witches there carry a contagious disease that causes purple spots, so most denizens of the forest do their best to avoid it. But I hear they serve an extraordinary chicken soup."

"That sounds delicious," Warren said. He was so hungry, even purple-spotted pimples seemed a fair price to pay for a good meal.

"And that way is Boar Rock," Sir Sap continued, pointing to the south. "It's a giant boulder that resembles a bristly hog, tusks and all. It was shaped by ancient witches who had the ability to warp stone. Sadly, rock-shaping is now a lost art. A lot of the older pieces have been destroyed, but Boar Rock still stands. It's made from one of the hardest stones on earth."

"Why would anyone want to destroy it?" Warren asked, perplexed.

"Because evil witches enjoy destruction," Sir Sap said, and a sad expression crossed his fuzzy face. "They have no appreciation for beauty. The lovelier something appears, the more they want to smash it to pieces."

Warren thought of his hotel and its many works of fine art. The most impressive gallery was the fifth-floor Hall of Ancestors [featuring portraits of thirteen generations of Warrens] but every floor had its own masterpieces: paintings of children with turnips for heads, statues of dancing lads and maidens, shy foxes, sprinting hounds, weeping cherubs. There were also grand tapestries in the game room depicting fantastical battles between knights and beasts, as well as cabinets filled with decorative vases and china, all painted with delicate pastoral scenes. If the witches gained entry to his hotel and saw all the beautiful and breakable things within . . . well, Warren didn't even want to think about what might happen.

After hours of walking, the pair finally paused for a break. Warren lay down to rest while Sir Sap walked around shaking trees, hoping to find one that was still full of sap. Sometimes Sir Sap would put his ear to the tree, almost as if listening to it.

"Are they saying anything?" Warren asked.

"Not right now," Sir Sap said.

"But you've heard them whisper at night?" Warren asked. "You do know what I'm talking about, right?"

"I have, indeed."

"If only there was a way to understand them," Warren said with a sigh. "Then we could simply ask why they stopped making sap."

"The trees speak an ancient language," Sir Sap said. He plopped onto a pile of leaves and plucked a thick twig from the ground. He began using his sharp claws to strip the bark, dejectedly. "Their words have been lost to time."

Warren wasn't ready to quit so easily.

"Maybe someone in the Malwoods will understand the chant," he said. "Maybe the witches understand it."

"No witch is going to help us," Sir Sap said.

Warren noticed that the wood in Sir Sap's paws was slowly beginning to take shape; he was transforming it from a twig into a tiny figure.

"What are you making?" Warren asked.

Sir Sap looked mildly embarrassed. "Nothing, really. It just helps take my mind off my hunger." He unfolded his paw to reveal a little wooden sap-squatch.

"That's amazing!" Warren said, highly impressed.

"Oh, this is just a rough little piece. I usually do much larger carvings."

"I'd love to see them!" Warren said.

Just then a shadow crossed Sir Sap's face. "I wish you could, but they were all destroyed when the witches enslaved my people."

"Oh," Warren said. He felt awful. Now he understood why Sir Sap seemed so sad when he explained how evil witches liked to destroy beautiful things.

"One day I'd like to open a toy shop," Sir Sap continued. "I promised my little sister I would."

"That would be neat!" Warren said. He had never been to a toy shop before, but he could imagine how wonderful it would be. He visualized a cozy room filled with rubber balls and dolls and toy cars and stuffed animals. Warren also imagined Sir Sap's wooden carvings lining the shelves: an entire army of sap-squatches waiting patiently for the loving embrace of a child.

Sir Sap stood and brushed leaves off his fur. "But right now I need to focus on getting sap to my people. My toy shop dreams will have to wait."

"Maybe it will happen sooner than you think," Warren said. "I always used to dream about managing the Warren Hotel, and then one day my dream came true."

Warren's voice trailed off as he remembered his current predicament. Sir Sap seemed to know what he was thinking, and he reached out to ruffle Warren's bushy hair. "We're both doing the best we can, and that's what matters. Now let's keep going so we can set things right again."

They continued on, both trying to ignore the rumbling in their stomachs. After about an hour, Sir Sap stopped abruptly, looking troubled.

"What's wrong?" Warren asked.

"There's a shortcut nearby—a bridge that spans a large river. If we cross it, we'll save ourselves the trouble of going around the long way."

"That sounds perfect," Warren said.

"Well, the downside is that the bridge is known to have a guardian. He might insist on a toll, and we have nothing to give him."

"Oh," Warren said. It seemed nothing was free in the Malwoods. "What's the toll?"

"That I do not know," Sir Sap said. "To be honest, I've always avoided the bridge. It has a rather sinister reputation."

That certainly didn't sound good. But Warren knew that a shortcut might be the only way to catch the hotel before it reached the Black Caldera. Sir Sap pointed the way and they continued onward for another hour or so, until the edges of a green, murky river came into view. It was the largest river Warren had ever seen—he couldn't even see the other side.

The bridge was equally impressive. It seemed to be knit from an assortment of bones in a way that reminded Warren of spiderwebs. But now that Warren saw the size of the river, he knew that walking around it wasn't an option—they had to cross the bridge, one way or another.

As they approached, Warren saw no sign of a guardian, and he dared to hope that they might be able to cross free of charge. "Hello?" he called out shakily. No reply. Warren wandered to the water's edge and even peered under the bridge, but there was only murky water drifting through the bridge's shadow.

"Maybe the guardian is just a myth," Warren said hopefully. "Let's try to cross and see what happens."

"You f-f-first!" Sir Sap said. To Warren's surprise, the mighty sap-squatch's voice was trembling.

Warren tentatively set one foot on the first rickety rung of the bone bridge.

Nothing happened.

But when he stepped on with his other foot, the bridge trembled and the earth shook. The surrounding water bubbled and frothed like a giant cauldron. "I knew this was a mistake," Sir Sap said. "Let's flee before it's too late!"

Warren was mesmerized as a large, roundish stone broke through the water's surface. The stone was studded with spiny bone-like protrusions, upon which stood a skeleton clad in rusty armor. Its eye sockets glowed an otherworldly hue.

"Who dares disturb our slumber?!" the skeleton roared. Its flinty voice sounded like thunder on a distant mountaintop. "We detest being awakened, for it will take us an eternity to return to sleep. The reason had better be worth our while, puny human!"

*Our?* That's when Warren realized that the stone the skeleton stood on was no stone at all but the hump of a giant tortoise. He could barely make out yellow reptilian eyes glowing beneath the water. Bubbles streamed up from leathery nostrils and burbled on the surface. Warren hoped the creature would stay where it was. The thing was large enough to eat him whole.

"I'm s-s-sorry," Warren stammered. "We just want to cross your bridge."

"And are you sure you can pay the price?" the guardian asked. "This bridge is constructed from the bones of those who have failed before you."

Warren looked at the bone bridge and swallowed hard.

"This is a bad idea," muttered Sir Sap.

Warren shook his head. He was determined to see it through. "What is it that you ask?"

"Only the answer to a riddle. Otherwise your bones will join the others."

"Oh no," Sir Sap moaned. "I'm terrible at puzzles!"

"I'm not," Warren said confidently. He turned to face the guardian. "What's the riddle?"

"Very well," the skeleton rumbled, and then he began to recite a poem:

*It can move you
like a demon
As if your body
were possessed.*

*It can be found on
deck with seamen,
And in a blue—
bird's nest.*

*Never whispered and
rarely screamed,
It's free but never cheap.*

*If you wish to cross
our bridge redeemed,
You'll put us
back to sleep.*

Warren closed his eyes and thought hard. What could make your body move as though possessed? Maybe shivers—either from cold or from fear. He supposed those could be found on the deck of a ship and in a bird's nest, but he didn't think that was the right answer. Shivers didn't fit with "never whispered and rarely screamed."

"I've got it!" Sir Sap cried suddenly.

"You do?" Warren asked.

"Yes, it's the flu!" Sir Sap said proudly. "The flu makes your body feel as though it were possessed, and sailors are known for getting sick at sea. And you could say a bluebird flew, which sounds the same!"

"That's a good guess," Warren admitted. "But would you say the flu is never whispered and rarely screamed? Would you say that it's free but never cheap?"

Sir Sap slumped his shoulders. "Hmm, I didn't think of that."

Down in the water, the giant tortoise snapped its beak, causing water to spray upward. "We grow weary of waiting!" the skeleton grumbled.

"Do you have the answer or not?"

Just as before in the tree, the solution suddenly struck Warren. The guardian and his tortoise were tired. They wished to be lulled back to sleep. And what better way than with a lullaby or, rather . . .

"A song!" Warren cried. "That's the answer!"

The earth rumbled again and the water frothed as the tortoise stirred. For a moment, Warren feared he was mistaken, but then he heard the sound of thunderous laughter.

"Very good, little boy. You've solved my riddle. You are the first to have done so in many months. I'm impressed."

"I'm impressed, too!" Sir Sap said. "I never would have thought of that!"

"So can we cross?" Warren asked.

"Not so fast," the guardian replied. "You've merely guessed the payment. Now you must pay."

"You mean, you want a song?" Warren said.

*"HOW ELSE DO YOU EXPECT US TO FALL ASLEEP?" THE SKELETON ASKED.*

"Excellent! I shall sing the sap-squatch anthem!" Sir Sap said, and he opened his jaw and let out a stream of horrible yowls. Warren winced.

# "SILENCE!"

the skeleton cried, covering what would have been his ears, had he possessed any. The tortoise stirred, churning the water like a boiling cauldron. "You call that howling a song? You'll pay for this insolence!"

"Wait!" Warren cried. "Let me have a try! I know just the thing—"

And before the guardian could object, Warren cleared his throat and began to sing:

"OH HO HO! JACQUES RUSTYBOOTS BE MY NAME!
TRAV'LING THE GLOBE BE MY CLAIM TO FAME!
NO MONSTER OF LAND, NOR AIR, NOR SEA
WILL EVER SUCCEED IN FRIGHT'NING ME!
FOR I BE CLEVER AND BRAVE AND STRONG!
AND WHEN COURAGE I NEED, I SING THIS SONG!"

He realized that he'd managed to get through the song without protest, so he repeated the lyrics, over and over, while Sir Sap provided a little dance. Soon the guardian's skull began to droop, and the tortoise's eyes slowly closed. Eventually the hump descended into the water, and the guardian disappeared beneath the surface with a final *BLORP*. Ripples spread outward and then the water stilled, as smooth as glass.

"We did it," Warren whispered.

"It appears so," said Sir Sap.

But even though the way forward seemed clear, they stepped cautiously onto the bridge, half-afraid the guardian's tortoise would surface again and chomp down on them with its powerful jaw.

The bridge was very long and rose to a great height at its apex. Stopping to rest there, Warren and Sir Sap took a moment to catch their breath. From this vantage, they could see for miles. Warren could make out his hotel, still stomping away in the east. It wasn't so far, and he felt a surge of hope that they could catch it before time ran out.

As Warren pulled away from the bridge's railing, he noticed something else. Etched on the bones were angular letters—the etchings were so faint, he hadn't noticed them. They read:

*Tolo lops sto yihop id stipf*

*baunm si vuxo ak:*

*Sto reqj, sto diirupt, ehz*

*stipf custias gicuo.*

*Stoj curr hoxol lowiuno uh dloozig.*

Warren showed the letters to Sir Sap. "What do you suppose they mean?"

Sir Sap tried to read the message but couldn't make any sense of it. "I have no idea," he said, "but here's one that's written in Sap-squatch." He reached for another bone covered in indecipherable symbols.

"And here's one in English!" Warren said, and he proceeded to read it aloud:

*Here rest the bones of those*

*quick to give up:*

*the lazy, the foolish, and*

*those without moxie.*

*They will never rejoice in freedom.*

"I didn't know you could read Sap-squatch!" Sir Sap exclaimed.

"I can't," Warren said.

"Well, that happens to be the exact translation of the Sap-squatch writing," Sir Sap said.

# "A-HA!"

Warren exclaimed. "So the warning is presented in three languages: one for humans, one for sap-squatches, and one for . . . whoever speaks this third language."

"One warning is plenty for me," Sir Sap said with a shudder. "Let's hurry to the other side. I don't like this bridge very much."

"Wait a minute," Warren said. "What if this third language is the ancient tongue of the trees?"

"That seems quite unlikely," Sir Sap said. "Why would a tree need to cross a bridge?"

Warren copied the three phrases in his sketchbook anyway. In a place as dangerous as the Malwoods, even the smallest bit of information could mean the difference between life and death.

CHAPTER XIII

IN WHICH

PETULA

ENCOUNTERS

A WITCH

ight was falling, Petula was exhausted, and even Sketchy seemed to be growing weary. Petula felt sorry for the creature—it was trying so hard to catch up with the hotel, but it was no match for the building's extraordinary mechanical speed.

"You've done well, Sketchy," she said, gently patting its side. "But it looks like we won't be reaching the hotel tonight and you need to rest. We'd better find a place to camp."

Hoping to avoid any evil beings who might be traveling on the road, Petula and Sketchy ventured into the forest, seeking a safe spot to settle. The problem was, no place felt safe. All around them were the sounds of creatures stirring and growling. Glowing eyes glared out from shadowy nooks. Ravenous insects swarmed around their faces, threatening to bite. And a surprising number of snakes slithered about.

To make matters worse, an eerie whisper echoed throughout the woods. It was spooky, though the voices seemed harmless. Petula tried to ignore them as she watched for stray witches. She had only one perfumier bottle tucked in her pocket, and it didn't feel like nearly enough.

"If only we could find some shelter," Petula said. "It's not safe to sleep out in the open." The words had barely left her mouth when a light rain began to fall. The sound of droplets sprinkling through the trees created a *HISSSSSSSS* that drowned out most other noises, including the whispers. But it also made it harder to hear signs of danger.

Sketchy didn't mind the rain and spun around happily, sprinkling droplets in every direction. Petula, however, did not relish the thought of spending the night drenched

in a puddle. As the sun fell, the temperature also dropped several degrees. Petula was wondering if they should try to build some sort of protection when she spotted a distant lamplight. "Sketchy, look!" she said, pointing to the yellow glow. "Let's go check it out."

Petula's senses remained on high alert as she and Sketchy crept through the foliage toward the light. It seemed warm and beckoning, but Petula knew that—like everything else in the Malwoods—something that appeared friendly could easily be a trap. As they drew closer, the light was revealed to be the glowing window of a little cottage. Hanging above the door was a wooden sign that read: "Hattie's Wig Shoppe and Haberdashery." *Seems harmless enough,* Petula thought, stroking her chin. Plus, her hair and dress were sopping wet, so a dry cottage was incredibly inviting.

"We'll just ask to spend the night," she told Sketchy. "Don't be alarmed, but I'm going to pretend to be an evil witch. I think it's the only way we'll get help in these parts."

Sketchy whistled softly, and Petula waved her arm, casting a glamour to appear as though she wore a long black cloak. The cowl cast a dark shadow over her face, making her seem even more mysterious. It was only an illusion—the cloak didn't offer warmth or keep her dry, but it did make her look sufficiently evil, which was all that mattered.

Together, they approached the cottage and Petula knocked on the door.

"I'm closed!" answered a cranky voice.

Petula breathed deeply and opened the door. Inside the shop was an elderly witch sitting near a counter. Her face was as wrinkled as a raisin, and her large brown eyes blinked owl-like behind thick glasses. A frizzy halo of gray hair stuck out in every direction, and she was dressed in a thick

shawl. Perched on a stool, she was using a wooden crochet hook to weave silky auburn strands into a cap.

On the wall behind her was a large oak shelving unit filled with wigs of all sorts. There were sleek black wigs, frizzy brown wigs, wavy violet wigs, and curly red wigs. There was also a large assortment of hats displayed throughout the room——fancy hats adorned with beads and feathers, and a good number of plain black witch hats as well, the kind with wide brims and pointy tips.

"I said I'm closed!" the witch snarled.

Petula mustered her most authoritative voice. "My minion and I need a place to sleep for the night."

"This isn't a hotel," the witch snapped. "It's a wig shop and my home. So get out!"

Petula hesitated, desperate to win over the shop owner. "It must be a lot of work, running a wig shop all by yourself," she said. "Perhaps we can help you in return for a night's lodging."

"I already have an assistant."

"I don't see one," Petula said.

"She's already gone home. Because, in case you hadn't noticed, I'm *CLOSED*!"

Petula was running out of ideas. So she decided to try flattery.

"You certainly have a lot of fine wigs," she said. "Perhaps I should switch up my look. What do you think?"

The witch's eyes brightened. "I may be closed, but I'll never say no to a sale! Which one are you interested in?"

"I'm not sure," Petula said. "Let me browse your selection." She wandered aimlessly around the store, feigning interest in each wig while Sketchy tried on a variety of styles. The hair looked ridiculous on the creature, and Petula couldn't help but smile. Then, remembering that she was supposed to be an evil witch, she forced herself to frown instead.

As she made her way through the selections, Petula noticed a magical broom hanging by a hook near the back door. It was made from a thick, sturdy branch—more than long enough to support both her and Sketchy. It would be the perfect vehicle to catch the hotel. But how could she convince the wig maker to part with it?

"Well," the witch demanded, "what have you decided?"

"I don't know . . . ," Petula said, trying to stall.

"Pull down your hood," the witch directed, "and let's see what we're working with." Petula obliged, and the witch seemed delighted, reaching out to touch a strand. "Your hair is white as snow!"

"I could go for something a little more colorful," Petula said. "You have some wonderful options."

"It seems a shame to cover up such lovely hair . . . ," the witch replied, still stroking Petula's hair. She stopped abruptly. "You know, I've changed my mind. You can spend the night after all."

"We can?"

"Yes, of course! I'm sorry I was so inhospitable. It's been a long and tiring day."

"Oh," said Petula, "well, thank you."

"Make yourself at home, dearie. I'll put on a kettle and fetch some spare bedding."

After the witch hurried off, Petula exchanged a look with Sketchy and shrugged. Before long, they were both snuggled into warm blankets on the floor near the fireplace, alongside steaming mugs of hot cocoa.

"Well, now, good night," the witch said. "I hope you both sleep well. I'm sure you have more travels planned for tomorrow, so it's best to get all the rest you can."

"Thank you," Petula said, her eyes drooping. She was too tired to even drink her cocoa, so she pushed the mug over to Sketchy, who accepted it happily. "You can have mine. I'm going to sleep."

Petula closed her eyes and promptly fell asleep. A few hours later she awakened to the sound of soft footsteps padding toward her. Blinking drowsily, Petula propped herself up on her elbows. The witch was creeping toward her—and carrying an enormous pair of scissors.

"Sketchy!" Petula cried. "Get up!"

But the monster lay stiff as stone.

The witch glared at Petula. "How are you still awake?" she demanded. "I put a freezing potion in your cocoa!" Then she leapt forward, scissors flashing in the glow of the dying fire. *Snip-snip-snip!*

Petula scooted backward, tripping over the hem of her robe and falling to the floor.

The witch fell upon her, scissors snipping, but Petula held her back with all the strength she could muster. The blades were mere inches from her face.

"If you wanted some of my hair," Petula grunted, "you could have just asked!"

"I don't want some!" the witch screeched.

## "I WANT IT ALL!"

Petula rolled sideways, flinging the witch to the floor and scrambling to her feet. Sketchy was still fast asleep, enchanted by the spell. The witch bounded up and ran after Petula, knocking her into the wall and sending a shelf full of mannequin heads toppling to the ground.

"YEOW!" Petula cried as the witch seized her hair and pulled hard. "Let go!" She summoned her zapping spell, which succeeded in throwing off the witch.

"Using magic now, are we?" the witch sneered. "Well I'll show YOU magic!"

Her wrinkled fingers did a strange little dance, as though they were weaving strands of air, and her hands blazed yellow. A magical blade of energy shot from her palms and sliced toward Petula's head.

But this time Petula was ready. She pulled out her bottle and uncorked it, and with a melting cry, the witch and her spell were sucked inside. Petula stumbled back, reeling from the force, and plugged the cork.

Almost immediately, Sketchy lifted its head and looked around; capturing the witch had broken the spell. Sketchy wriggled back to life and rushed over to Petula, chirping excitedly.

"I did it!" Petula cried. "I caught my first witch! All on my own!"

She watched in astonishment as a rose tattoo magically appeared on the back of her left hand—her casting hand. Sketchy clapped its tentacles and pulled her into a hug.

Petula felt a confidence she hadn't felt since her mom was taken prisoner. She was on her way to becoming a true perfumier!

# CHAPTER XIV

# IN WHICH

# WARREN

# BREAKS THE

# CODE

arren realized that the chief benefit of traveling with a sap-squatch was that all the other creatures gave them a wide berth. That was particularly handy when the rain started to fall and they were forced to seek shelter for the night.

"That cave looks promising," Sir Sap said, gesturing to a cavern in a nearby hillside that overlooked the river. His fur was drenched, and he emitted the rather unfortunate odor of wet dog.

Warren was desperate to find shelter, but he was nervous about entering another creature's home. "What if something's already living inside?"

"Oh, I wouldn't worry about that," Sir Sap said. He lumbered up to the entrance, poked his head inside, and growled threateningly. Within seconds, a flock of startled bats burst out of the darkness and flapped off into the night, leaving the cave empty.

# "ALL SET!"

Warren felt a little sorry for the displaced bats, but he was quite relieved to have a dry place in which to spend the night.

"I'll forage for food," Sir Sap said. "This area has patches of delicious berries."

"I'll start a fire," Warren said. "We'll be toasty and dry in no time!"

Even though most of his supplies had been lost in the quicksand, Warren had kept a box of matches safe in a pocket. Before long a cheerful fire was crackling near the mouth of the cave. Then Warren set himself to his other tasks, just as he would at the hotel: he swept the floor of the cave with a pine branch, made a bed for Sir Sap from a pile of dry leaves, and found a short log to serve as a pillow. If only he had a mint to place on top.

Sir Sap returned several minutes later, his paws full of berries and other edibles. And since his paws were quite large, their meal was big too.

"I've made the room ready for you," Warren said. "I hope you enjoy your stay."

"It looks wonderful!" Sir Sap exclaimed. Then his smile faded and he looked at Warren oddly. "Forgive me for asking but... why are you so nice? I've never met anyone quite like you."

Warren blushed. "That's how I was raised. My father taught me that serving other people is one of the most important things we can do."

"You don't see a lot of kindness in the Malwoods," Sir Sap said.

"That's not true," Warren said. "You're kind. You're trying to help your fellow sap-squatches. And one day you're going to build an incredible toy shop."

Now it was Sir Sap's turn to blush. He unloaded the food onto the ground and quickly changed the subject. "Well, it was my father who taught me that these are edible. Though I must warn you, they taste atrocious."

It was true—the roots and leaves and fruits formed a bitter and foul-tasting salad, but Warren was too hungry to care. Meanwhile, Sir Sap finished the last of his sap. He looked mournfully at the empty bottle and said, "Well, that's the end. Who knows when my next meal will be."

"Soon!" Warren said, pulling out his sketchbook. "Especially if I can decode these symbols."

As Warren puzzled over the code, Sir Sap stretched out by the fire and began carving tiny sculptures using the kindling that Warren had gathered. Before long a cluster of little sap-squatch statues were lined up by the fire.

After a while, Sir Sap fell asleep. He snored loudly, and it reminded Warren of his uncle Rupert, whose wheezing and snuffling could be heard throughout the hotel. Warren missed him.

He decided to distract himself by focusing on the words from the bridge that he had recorded in his sketchbook. The first was in his own language:

*Here rest the bones of those quick to give up:*
*the lazy, the foolish, and those without moxie.*
*They will never rejoice in freedom.*

And the second was in the ancient language:

*Tolo lops sto yihop id stipo baunm si vuxo ak:*
*Sto reqj, sto diirupt, ehz stipo fustias gicuo.*
*Stoj furr hoxol lowiuno uh dloozig.*

Eventually Warren realized that by matching the letters from each passage, he was able to come up with a key:

A B C D E F G H I J
E Y N Z O D V T U W
K L M N O P Q R S T
M R G H I K B L P S
U V W X Y Z
A X F C J Q

He double-checked his work and nodded, pleased with his discovery. Now it was time for the fun part: decoding the message that was whispered through the woods.

CODE KEY:

TORK AP!
IAL LIISP ROEZ
SI STO NERZOLE
IAL PEK DRIFP
SI STO BAOOH
FO ELO SLEKKOZ
DLOO AP

_ _ _ _  _ _!
_ _ _ _ _  _ _ _ _ _
_ _ _ _ _  _ _ _ _
_ _ _ _ _  _ _ _
_ _ _ _ _  _ _ _ _
_ _ _ _ _  _ _ _
_ _ _ _

Bit by bit, Warren swapped out the letters using his key. And as he did so, a message was revealed:

*Help us!*
*Our roots lead to the caldera*
*Our sap flows to the queen*
*We are trapped*
*Free us!*

Warren was astonished. All this time, the trees weren't threatening or warning him to stay out of the forest. They were asking for help! He was tempted to awaken Sir Sap immediately and share the good news, but he decided to wait. The sap-squatch needed his sleep, and the hotel manager in Warren was loath to disturb a guest.

Glancing out of the mouth of the cave, Warren saw that the rain had stopped. Perhaps this was his chance to talk to the trees and get some answers. He grabbed his sketchbook and hurried outside. He needed to walk several yards from the cave, since the fire was still glowing brightly within.

Finally, Warren was far enough into the darkness that the whispers returned in full force. Now that he understood what the trees were chanting, he could sense their urgency and frustration.

"I hear you, trees of the forest," Warren called out. "Tell me what I need to do to get your sap back!"

The whispers seemed to ignore his appeal, continuing to chant the same plea over and over. Realizing that he needed to speak in their language, Warren flipped open his sketchbook and translated what he wanted to say.

He repeated his plea, this time in the language of the whispering trees: "U toel jia! Sloop id sto dilops! Waps sorr go ftes U hooz si zi vos jail pek yenm."

The whispering silenced for a moment and Warren knew they had heard him. All at once, the pines seemed to tremble, their soft boughs hissing as needles vibrated against one another. They seemed . . . energized.

Perhaps even excited!

The whispering started again, only this time with a new chant. Warren hastily wrote the words in his sketchbook, then translated them into English:

You are a little boy and still quite young
But your true self is bigger and braver
To reveal the truth within,
Look into a mirror,
Say "rorrim,"
and the heart will be reflected!

Warren winced. He didn't particularly appreciate the comment about his size, but he was pleased with his progress. He shut his sketchbook and trudged back to the cave. At least in the morning he'd have good news for Sir Sap. The trees might not have offered a solution, but now he knew the queen was responsible for the sap shortage. Somehow she was controlling all the roots in the forest, forcing them to lead to the Black Caldera and draining their sap. *Well, not for long*, Warren thought. He clenched a fist and vowed to save not only his friends, but the trees as well.

All he needed was a plan.

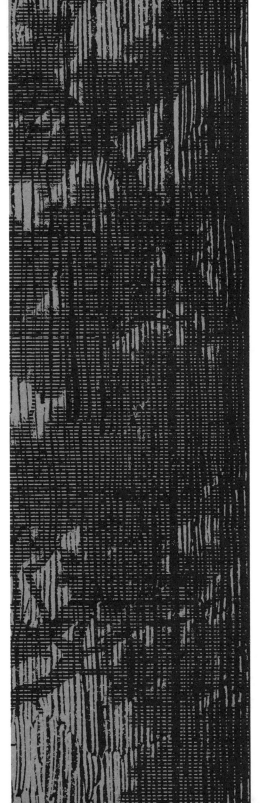

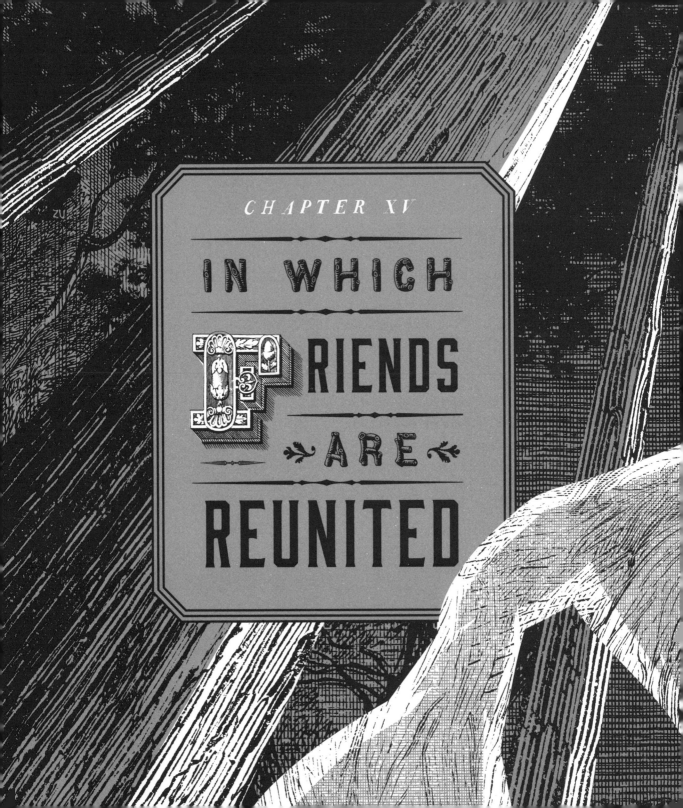

CHAPTER XV

IN WHICH

FRIENDS

ARE

REUNITED

he following morning, Warren told Sir Sap what he had learned. "Now that we know all of the sap is flowing to the queen, we just need to figure out where she's hiding it."

"That will be difficult," Sir Sap said, scratching his furry chin. "The queen is the most powerful witch in the Malwoods, and the Black Caldera contains an entire village of her most evil devotees. I don't see how we can sneak past all of them."

"Well, we won't accomplish anything by staying here and wondering," Warren said. "Let's get going!"

So Warren and Sir Sap set off, energized by the task ahead. They walked briskly, and before long the terrain became even hillier, with less vegetation and sparser trees. As they crested a hill, Warren could see the basin known as the Black Caldera and, just beyond it, the glittering ocean.

The crater was about a mile wide and surrounded by stone cliffs fifty feet tall, except for one section in which a giant doorway was carved; the door was flanked by gargantuan stone statues of witches holding staffs. Purple and green smoke rose from the crater, obscuring whatever lay within, but Warren could discern the dark shapes of witches on brooms as they darted in and out of the haze.

Warren could also see his hotel to the west, marching down the road that led to the mouth of the Black Caldera. "There it is!" Warren said, pointing. "My hotel will reach the caldera soon. I need to get back on board before it does!"

But how? Warren was still miles away from home, and without a vehicle like Sly's jalopy, there was no way he could move fast enough.

"Come on!" Warren said, tugging on Sir Sap's arm. "We have to hurry!"

They ran as fast as they could down the hill, trying not to trip over stones and logs dotting their path. Warren felt a little nervous—there were few trees around to cover them, and plenty more witches were zooming around.

Sure enough, the shadow of a flying witch passed overhead, and Warren heard a sharp whistle. He instinctively ducked and fell to the ground, expecting a spell to blast him at any moment.

Instead he heard a familiar voice: "Warren?"

"Petula?!" he cried in astonishment and looked up to see his friend and beloved pet Sketchy clinging to a broom that hovered overhead. Sketchy looked terrified; the creature's tentacles were wrapped tightly around both Petula and the broom handle. Petula steered downward and landed roughly beside him, sending her and Sketchy sprawling. The broom clattered lifelessly to the ground.

"Oof!" she said. "I'm still getting the hang of that thing."

Sketchy let out a shaky tweet as a tentacle wiped its brow.

"What are you doing here?" Petula and Warren asked each other in unison.

They both tried explaining at once, but in their excitement their voices overlapped. "Hold on, hold on!" Sir Sap said, interrupting the babble. "One at a time!"

Petula nearly shrieked. "A sap-squatch!"

"Yes, and it's a great pleasure to meet you," Sir Sap said, shaking Petula's hand. She blinked in astonishment at his impeccable manners.

"My name is Petula," she said. "I'm a friend of Warren's." Then she looked at Warren and cried, "You need to know something! There's a mimic at the hotel who's impersonating you!"

"I know!"

"You—you know?"

"Yes! I've been trying to catch the hotel so I can stop him!"

Petula went on to explain that her

mother had been captured by Queen Calvina's coven. "She's somewhere in the Black Caldera, and I'm going to free her."

"You're in luck," Warren said. "Sir Sap is from the caldera, so he knows his way around."

Warren then went on to tell her about the sap shortage, and how the queen was holding the sap-squatches prisoner as well.

"I think I've made a pretty good plan," Warren said. "Once I get inside the hotel and defeat the mimic, I'll use the building to storm the Black Caldera and create a diversion. That will give you a chance to save your mom, and then Sir Sap can find where all the sap is going."

"You mean, you'll allow the witches to attack the hotel?" Petula cried in alarm.

"The hotel was built for battle," Warren reminded her. "It can handle it."

"It's an excellent distraction," Sir Sap said. "Once I release the sap, my fellow sap-squatches will be strong enough to fight and overthrow the witches so that you and your hotel can escape."

"Okay, let's do it," Petula said, and Sketchy wiggled excitedly.

"Can I use this to fly to the hotel?" Warren asked, picking up the broom.

"It won't work unless you're a witch," Petula said. "I'll take you." She turned to Sir Sap and said, "You start heading toward the caldera. I'll find you after I drop off Warren."

"Then we'll sneak into the caldera together," Sir Sap said. "I know of a hidden entrance!"

"What about Sketchy?" Warren asked.

"There's not enough room for all three of us on the broom," Petula said.

Warren patted Sketchy on the back. "Sketchy, can you go with Sir Sap and help him find the missing sap?"

Sketchy whistled and tapped its head.

"That means yes," Petula explained.

"Then it's settled!" Warren said. "Let's go!"

"One moment," Sir Sap said, looking bashful. "Before we say farewell, I wanted to give you this. Just in case I never see you again."

He handed Warren a little carving. It was a perfect miniature replica of the Warren Hotel.

"Now you'll always have your home with you," Sir Sap said, "should you ever find yourself lost again."

Warren blinked away tears and hugged Sir Sap. "Thank you! I'll consider it my personal good-luck charm. And I need all the luck I can get."

Without further ado, Petula hopped onto the broom, which instantly lifted off the ground. "Ready?" she asked. Warren nodded and climbed on behind her. "Be safe, Sir Sap! You, too, Sketchy!"

The broom took off like a rocket and Warren couldn't help but let out a "Waahoo!" as they shot into the sky.

"Hold on tight!" Petula said. "This broom doesn't seem to like me too much."

Sure enough, Warren could feel the broom resist, bucking several times like a wild horse.

"How high can we go?" he asked.

"There's only one way to find out," Petula said. They soared higher and higher until the hotel looked small as a bug. From above the clouds, Warren could see the distant plains to the west, where he had started his journey, and the obstacles he had faced along the way: the top of the talking oak and the pool of quicksand and the bone bridge over the murky river. *I walked all that way,* he thought in amazement.

Looking over his other shoulder, Warren could see down into the Black Caldera, with all its little huts and Queen Calvina's sprawling palace made of bones. But one building especially stood out. On its roof was painted a strange symbol.

"Do you see that?" Warren asked, pointing at the hut. "I wonder what that symbol means."

"It could be some kind of magical ward to protect the building from spells," Petula said. "Maybe that's where the sap is being stored."

"We should certainly check," Warren said, making a mental note of the building's location.

Petula tilted the broomstick and they began their descent toward the hotel.

She steered to the front door, taking care to match the hotel's speed so that they wouldn't be crushed by the building's forward momentum.

Warren hopped off the broom and onto the porch. "Thanks, Petula! Good luck!"

"You too, Warren!" Petula said. "Remember to go see Mr. Friggs right away!"

Warren nodded and waved as she zipped off to rejoin Sir Sap. Then he pressed his ear to the front door and listened, making sure that no one was in the lobby. He couldn't hear anything, so he slowly eased open the door and peeped through the crack.

The lobby was empty.

He stepped inside, quietly pulling the door closed behind him. He crept across the checkered floor toward the staircase, knowing that any noise would echo loudly in the cavernous lobby. He had reached the staircase when he heard his Uncle Rupert's voice cry out:

Warren froze. It sounded as though it had come from the dining hall. Uncle Rupert was in trouble!

Warren instantly changed course and ran down the side hallway to the ballroom, skidding to a stop just outside the doors. He knew he shouldn't barge in—he wasn't even sure what he was dealing with.

With heart pounding, Warren gently pushed the door only an inch or so to avoid causing the old hinges to squeak. He pressed his eye to the opening, fully expecting a horrific scene. Instead he saw Uncle Rupert, Chef Bunion, and Mr. Vanderbelly all sitting around the dining table eating dinner with the mimic, Worrin. The air was filled with the fragrant aromas of baked ham and mashed potatoes. Rupert stretched his arm across the wooden surface, reaching for a gravy boat just beyond his grasp. Again he cried out, "HELP!"

"Oh, for heaven's sake," Mr. Vanderbelly muttered.

But Worrin leapt to his feet, grabbing the gravy boat and carrying it to Uncle Rupert. "It's no problem, Mr. Vanderbelly," he said sweetly. "Nothing brings me more joy than meeting all of my uncle's needs!"

Rupert smiled gratefully. "You're a good boy, Warren," he said. "The best nephew a man could ask for!"

Warren almost choked. For years he'd been running the hotel while his Uncle

Rupert loafed about, and he'd never received any such compliment. Could it be that Uncle Rupert preferred Worrin to Warren?

"He's certainly the best hotel manager I've ever met!" Chef Bunion said. "Let's raise a glass to Warren! He keeps cool under pressure and keeps us all safe from danger!"

"Hear, hear!" Mr. Vanderbelly cheered, holding up a glass.

"Please, stop!" Worrin said. "You're making me blush!"

"You deserve our praise," Chef Bunion said firmly.

"I agree!" Mr. Vanderbelly added. "I've always admired the service here, but since entering the Malwoods it has been absolutely outstanding. Truly, you're the best

hotel manager I've ever met!"

Warren felt sick. All this time, he imagined that the imposter was ruining his hotel. He'd fully expected to find his friends in peril. Instead, they seemed happier than ever. They loved Worrin.

*Maybe Worrin is a better hotel manager*, Warren thought glumly. He tried to shake off those feelings. Nothing changed the fact that he needed to defeat the mimic and reclaim his hotel. But first he had to find Mr. Friggs.

Warren wasted no time scurrying up to the fourth floor, pausing when he heard footfalls receding.

"Mr. Friggs?" he asked aloud. "Is that you?"

No response. Perhaps it was just a rat

scurrying over the floorboards. Warren continued to the library and was surprised to find the door locked.

"Mr. Friggs?" he said, banging on the door. "It's me, Warren!"

"Go away!" came a voice from the other side.

"No, it's the real me!" Warren insisted. "Not the mimic!"

"I'm not opening this door!"

"Please, Mr. Friggs. I need your help!"

"I said, GO AWAY!"

Warren reeled. His mentor had never spoken to him so cruelly. He realized that Mr. Friggs didn't care that he was back. Perhaps he preferred the mimic, too.

Warren left the library and trudged back down the hall. If no one wanted him around, maybe he should just leave.

"It's my own fault," Warren said bitterly. "I was foolish enough to lose my hotel. Maybe I don't deserve to keep it."

With a heavy heart, he walked down one floor to the Hall of Ancestors, where portraits of all of his forefathers hung in a neat row down a long hallway. The flickering candlelight seemed to animate the Warrens' faces, and he nodded respectfully to each one as he made his way past. Often he felt as though the paintings were windows through which the spirits of his relatives peered, sometimes approvingly and sometimes scornfully. Right now Warren couldn't help but think it was the latter.

But his father's portrait, which hung at the end of the row, always looked patient and kind. Seeing the gentle expression in Warren the 12th's eyes only made Warren the 13th feel worse.

"Dad," he said, "I've failed the hotel and I've failed you. I'm sorry, but I'm giving up. No one wants me around anymore. The guests have all gone, and even my friends are happier without me. It's for the best."

• WARREN THE 12TH •

He waited a moment, hoping to recall one of his father's lessons or sayings. But nothing came to mind. Perhaps even his own dad had turned his back on him. Warren looked at the framed artwork hanging next to the likeness. It was a family portrait that Warren had drawn, featuring him and all his friends in the happy days after he discovered the hotel could walk, when everything seemed possible. He wished he could get that feeling back.

Long before the drawing, a mirror had hung there, and he would often look at it and imagine his own portrait next to his father's. The mirror was now on the opposite side of the hall, and when Warren turned to look at it, he could see his father's portrait reflected in the glass. Still watching. Still smiling.

As for Warren the 13th, he looked tired and dirty from all his travels—not at all how the manager of a fine hotel should look. "Beauty is on the inside," his father used to say. "As long as you have a good heart, that's all that matters."

Warren realized that advice sounded familiar. He reached for his sketchbook and flipped to the page on which he'd decoded the trees' second message:

*You are a little boy and still quite young*
*But your true self is bigger and braver*
*To reveal the truth within,*
*Look into a mirror,*
*Say "rorrim,"*
*and the heart will be reflected!*

Curious, Warren glanced back at the mirror. He spoke the magic word *rorrim* and was shocked to see the surface shimmer and ripple like water. Suddenly, his reflection began to change; he grew taller, older, more confident, courageous even! In this new reflection, Warren saw that he looked just like his dad.

*It's me on the inside,* he realized. *It's my true heart reflected!*

Almost as soon as the image had appeared it faded away, and Warren was left looking at his regular self: a short, bug-eyed little boy. Yet something stirred within him. He knew that he had a courageous heart. What kind of boy with a good heart would abandon his family's hotel and all his friends in a time of need? Beatrice still needed to be saved, and Petula and Sketchy were out there risking their lives to find her. He couldn't leave them to fight this battle alone.

Warren turned back to his father's portrait. "Thanks, Dad."

He finally knew what he had to do.

CHAPTER

IN WHICH
WARREN

LXVI

CHAPTER XVI

BATTLES
WORRIN

arren returned to the library and banged on the door again.

"Mr. Friggs!" he said loudly. "I know you're afraid, but we're all in danger and I need your help before the hotel reaches the Black Caldera!"

"You're just trying to deceive me!" Mr. Friggs called back. "Petula warned me not to open the door for anyone!"

Warren thought hard. How could he convince Mr. Friggs that he was the real Warren?

with flowers. Mr. Friggs and Chef Bunion were in attendance, as well as hotel guests who were fond of the boy. Balloons were strung from the animal-shaped topiaries that dotted the grounds. Warren's gift was a small leather-bound sketchbook and a tin filled with watercolor paints.

"He told me, 'Never forget that a hotel has as much room for friendships as it has rooms. This means you'll always have friends to count on, no matter what life may bring.'"

## "I CAN PROVE IT!"

Warren said. "Ask me a question that only the real Warren could answer."

"Very well," Mr. Friggs said after a long moment. "Tell me: what did your father say to you at your seventh birthday party?"

Warren remembered it well. His eyes grew misty as he recalled the small party his father had staged on the grassy lawn outside the hotel. In those days, the grass was beautifully manicured and brimming

Warren heard the sound of a turning lock, and the door opened.

Mr. Friggs's eyes glistened with tears. "It is you!" He pulled Warren into a strong embrace. "What happened? Tell me every-thing!" he said, locking the door behind them and hobbling to his desk. Warren obliged, launching into a hurried explanation of everything that had happened up to that point.

"I need to defeat the mimic and retake control of the hotel before it reaches the Black Caldera," Warren said. "Do you know if he has any weaknesses?"

Mr. Friggs dropped a thick book onto his desk. The title on the cover read CREATURES OF THE DARK: FAERIES, GOBLINS, AND TROLLS, AS WELL AS ASSORTED OTHER MAGICKAL PESTS.

"You're in luck," he said. "I've been up all night researching, and I've found just the thing." He thumbed through the yellowed pages and landed on a section titled "MIMIC [see also DOPPELGANGER AND FETCH]."

"Did he take something from you in order to transform?"

"Yes, my tooth!" Warren said.

"Then you must get it back. The tooth is sustaining the illusion."

"That's going to be tricky," Warren said. "It's in his mouth."

"I'm afraid that's the easy part," Mr. Friggs said. "Once you have the tooth, he'll revert to his true form, and that's when your difficulties will begin. A mimic can haunt and torment a person as long as it pleases. Some people are driven mad by vengeful mimics that refuse to let them be. The only way to vanquish it is to speak its true name."

"But I don't know its true name."

"You will need to find it out," Mr. Friggs said. "And I believe that if anyone can do it, it's you."

"Thank you, Mr. Friggs," Warren said, giving his mentor another hug. "Stay here where it's safe. I have a feeling things are about to get pretty crazy."

Warren left Mr. Friggs in the library and stepped out into the hall. He felt nervous, but he had no time to dwell. He looked out the nearest window and saw the Black Caldera in the distance. They were getting close, and Warren knew he needed to deal with Worrin alone. But how?

Luring Worrin away from Uncle Rupert and Chef Bunion was essential. Warren wouldn't dare confront the mimic if it meant putting his friends in jeopardy. He walked over to the intercom in the wall, cleared his throat, and pressed the button. In a high-pitched voice he said, "Warren! This is Petula. Can you meet me in the attic, please?"

Even disguised, Warren's voice sounded nothing like Petula's, but he hoped the static would make it less obvious. In any case, he knew the mimic would take the bait. Warren scurried up the stairs and pulled down the ladder leading to the attic.

He was relieved to find that his room was exactly as he'd left it. The walls were covered with his drawings, along with doodles and scribbles by Sketchy. The bed was still made, and his few belongings were stacked in a neat pile on the nightstand: his Jacques Rustyboots books, a shoe polish kit, and a bag of marbles.

Warren remembered how his evil Aunt Annaconda had forced him to live in the small out-of-the-way space when she first moved in to the hotel. Now that she was gone and he was manager, Warren could have claimed any chamber in the hotel for himself. But he decided to stay in the attic. He had grown to like it. It was his home.

He heard the stomp of angry footsteps fast approaching and took a deep, steadying breath. This is my turf, he reminded himself.

"Petula!" Worrin shouted as he clambered up the ladder. "You have some nerve coming back to the hotel! I'm going to—" Worrin poked his head through the trap door, saw Warren standing in the room, and froze. "You!" he gasped. "What are *you* doing here?"

"This is my hotel," Warren said. "And you've stolen my identity!"

"I think not," the mimic said. "I'm minutes away from delivering this hotel to the queen and claiming my reward. I'm not letting anything stand in my way!"

With a flicker of dark magic, Worrin doubled and redoubled himself two, four,

eight, sixteen times, until Warren found himself completely encircled by duplicates. *Don't be afraid,* he told himself. *They're just illusions.*

But then the ring of Worrins stepped forward, seizing Warren with their cold hands. Illusion or not, they certainly felt real!

"It is time for you to vacate the premises," they said in unison, carrying him up the ladder to the roof. Warren struggled but couldn't free himself from their grasp. Once on the rooftop, the Worrins stomped to the edge, preparing to toss Warren over the side.

"Wait!" Warren cried. "Let's make a deal!"

"What could you possibly offer us?" the Worrins said with a sneer.

*The mimic is greedy,* Warren realized. *I just have to figure out what it wants.*

"I'll double whatever reward the queen has promised you!"

The Worrins laughed, producing a rather unsettling effect. "Impossible!" they said. "Unless you can give us twice our heart's desire! Only the queen has the power to make us a somebody!"

A notion tickled the back of Warren's brain, but he pushed it aside and said, "But you already are a somebody! From what I've seen, you're quite a good hotel manager. All of the staff seems to like and respect you. That's your proof right there."

The mimics paused; their magic seemed to falter. "Do you really think that's true?" they asked.

"I'm sure it's true!" Warren exclaimed.

They set Warren down gently and then merged once again. "I suppose you're right," the single Worrin said. "I've never had friends until now, nor an uncle of my own. But now that I'm managing the hotel, I really am somebody."

"But if you hand the hotel over to the queen," Warren said, "she'll take that away from you. She wants the Warren Hotel for herself. Do you think she'd really let you stay and run things? No way!"

The mimic frowned. "I hadn't thought of that."

"So let's make a deal," Warren said. "If you give me my tooth, I'll sign over the deed to the hotel."

The mimic looked puzzled. "The deed?"

"Yes, having the deed makes you the rightful owner. If you want to be a somebody, you'll need that deed, for sure."

"All right, it's a deal," the mimic said.

Warren reached for his sketchbook. "I'll draw up a contract right now."

On a fresh page, he wrote out the terms of their agreement.

"Now the tooth, if you please."

The mimic looked at him suspiciously. "This better not be a trap."

Warren snapped the sketchbook shut. "Are you saying you've changed your mind?"

"No, no! A deal's a deal," Worrin said quickly. It reached into its mouth and yanked out the tooth. In a swirl of darkness, the mimic's appearance washed away like smoke over glass. In Worrin's place stood a squat, shadowy creature that held Warren's tooth between vaporous fingers.

Warren found it difficult to look directly at the creature; its form flickered and shifted, like a trick of the eyes. Warren held out his palm and the mimic dropped the tooth into his grasp. Warren quickly put it in his pocket. Step one complete!

"Now, give me the deed!" the mimic said.

"Of course," Warren said. "Now I just need you to sign the contract and make it all official."

The mimic took the pencil and placed the tip on the page where "X" marked the spot. Warren held his breath. But rather than writing a name, the mimic growled low. A loud *SNAP!* sounded as the pencil broke in half.

"You're trying to figure out my name," it hissed. "You tricked me!"

"You're the one who stole my tooth!" Warren countered.

The mimic snarled in fury and seemed to grow larger in rage. Within seconds its shadowy figure loomed over Warren, blocking out the light. Warren gasped as the blackness expanded; soon he couldn't see anything, not even his own hands in front of his face. A chilling cold filled his bones and spread outward, inching across his skin. He shivered and whirled around, but no matter which way he turned, all he saw was black.

"You dare trick me? I will haunt you forever!" the mimic cried. "I will make your life a daily misery! Now you will see how it feels to be a mimic!"

Warren still couldn't see anything, but suddenly he could feel the mimic's pain, its loneliness and desperation. Tears stung his eyes as he recalled his own loneliness, his sorrow at being orphaned, his fear of being rejected by everyone he cared about.

Then he was struck by a memory.

*I wasn't always a tree, you know.*

The memory of the talking oak.

*But I grew tired of being a nobody, always imitating, always pretending to be someone I wasn't.*

The tree used to be a mimic, too, Warren realized. All at once, he knew how to defeat Worrin.

"I know your true name!" he yelled.

"Impossible!" the mimic cried back.

"The reason you mimic others is because you don't have an identity or a body of your own," Warren said. "That means you're—"

"STOP! SAY NO MORE!" the mimic screamed.

In its fear and anger, the mimic's darkness pressed around Warren, filling him with a soulless dread. A cold wind swirled around him, stinging his face and throwing daggers of chill across his body. But Warren gritted his teeth and pushed through the fear.

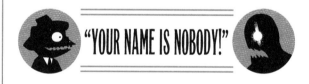

"YOUR NAME IS NOBODY!"

The mimic howled in agony. Warren was struck by one final blast of icy wind, which caused him to huddle against its sheer force. Just as it grew unbearably cold, the wind died down and the darkness dissipated. Warren could see the mimic crouching in the middle of the roof, dissolving into smoke.

And then it faded away forever.

CHAPTER XVII

In Which
PETULA
Enters the
BLACK CALDERA

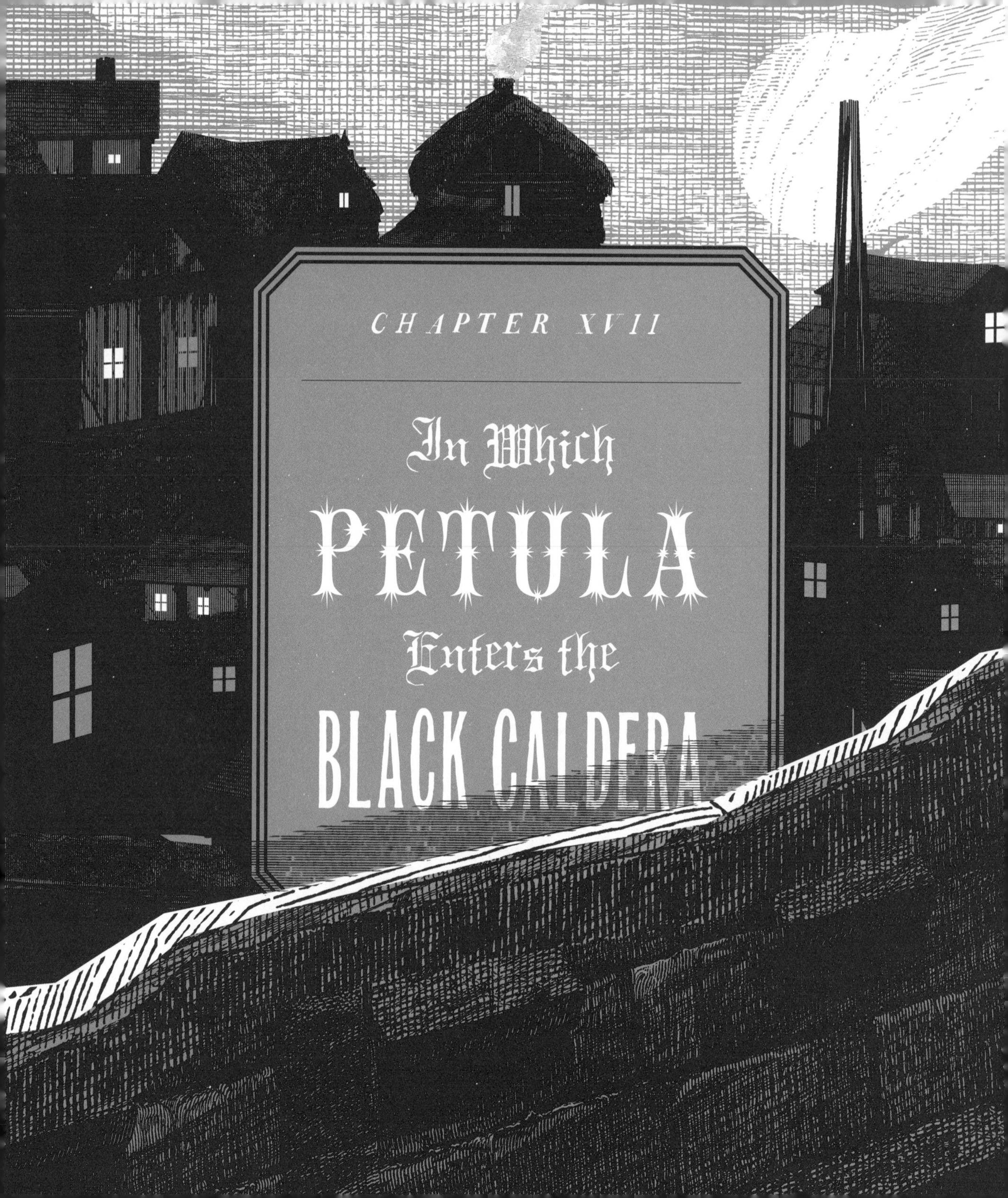

ollow me," Sir Sap said to Petula and Sketchy.

On either side, the earth sloped into tall cliffs and the road was steep and choked with stones and thorns. At the very end, the tall walls of the Black Caldera loomed; just seeing them made Petula pick up her pace.

"Wait!" Sir Sap cried. "Look!"

He pointed to the witches standing guard near the entrance—at least ten of them, all with beetle-black eyes and sharp-looking fingernails. "We're never going to get past them," Petula said with a groan. "Didn't you say there was a hidden entrance?"

"Yes," Sir Sap said. "It's right next to the main door. See that boulder there? It's blocking a tunnel that leads through underground passages."

"How do we get inside without them seeing us?"

"We just have to wait for a distraction," Sir Sap said. "And I believe there's one coming along right now. Listen!"

Petula tilted her head, and there it was: the distant *CLANG! CLANG! CLANG!* of the Warren Hotel's approaching footsteps. The guards cheered its arrival.

"The hotel is coming!" they screeched. "Alert the queen!"

*I sure hope Warren has everything under control,* Petula thought.

"Now's our chance," Sir Sap whispered.

On the count of three, Petula, Sketchy, and Sir Sap dashed toward the giant rock. It looked even bigger up close. Sir Sap pushed on it with his furry shoulder but it wouldn't budge. "It's heavier than I thought," he said. "Maybe I just need to take a running start—"

"No!" Petula cried, but she was too late. Sir Sap took two giant steps backward, his big fuzzy form directly in view of the witches.

"Hey!" A shrill voice rang out over the path. "What's going on over there?"

A blast of purple lighting exploded. The guard witch was coming after them, tearing up the path with another spell swirling around her.

Petula's heart leapt into her throat. "Sir Sap, do something!"

The sap-squatch threw his body against the boulder, but it simply wouldn't budge.

"I'm trying!" he said.

Something jabbed urgently at Petula's back. It was Sketchy—or rather a tentacle, which it used to nudge her and Sir Sap aside. Then the beast wrapped its tentacle around the boulder and, with a mighty whistle, heaved it out of the way.

The three of them ducked into the passage and Sketchy yanked the boulder back just in time, sealing them in darkness as another lightning blast hit. The witch's cries were silenced behind the thick barrier.

"Great work, Sketchy!" Petula said.

The creature whistled happily: *No problem!*

"Oh dear," Sir Sap said shakily.

"What's wrong?" Petula whispered.

Sir Sap wrung his hands. "It's quite silly, really, but . . . I'm afraid I'm scared of the dark!"

Petula smiled. Now that was something her magic could handle. With a wave of a hand, she created a soft glow that filled the tunnel with light. "Is that better?"

"Much," Sir Sap said gratefully. "Onward!"

The corridor ahead of them was deep, dark, and dank. Petula did her best to lead the way, but there were so many twists and turns, she couldn't be sure they were going in the right direction.

Besides, she realized that the farther underground they ventured, the farther they'd have to come up to reach the caldera and find Beatrice.

"This is awfully convoluted," Petula said. "Are you sure it's the right way?"

They had passed smaller corridors, but Sir Sap ignored them as he led them on.

"It's probably confusing on purpose," Sir Sap said. "Though I admit it's possible we took a wrong turn."

"Possible?" Petula said with growing dread. "Or positive?"

Sir Sap stopped. "We may be lost."

Sketchy let out a shrill whistle that echoed off the tunnel walls, again and again and again, as if to show just how far they'd gone.

"Stay calm," Sir Sap said. "There's no use panicking."

And so they carried on, the ground getting steeper and the walls getting closer. They wouldn't be lost forever, Petula knew—she could always portal herself out of the tunnel—but Sketchy was too big to fit through, and Sir Sap would probably struggle, too. Regardless, Petula refused to even think of leaving until she'd found her mother.

Sketchy stopped abruptly, licked the tip of a tentacle, and raised it in the air with a curious chirp.

"A draft!" Sir Sap exclaimed. "I feel it, too. And look, my fur is ruffling!"

Petula understood. "We must be near an exit!"

They nearly ran through the labyrinthine corridor until it dead-ended at a solid stone wall.

"Oh, what a cruel trick," Sir Sap cried in dismay.

"No, look!" Petula said, pointing up to a round metal grate. "It's some kind of trapdoor."

Once again Sketchy saved the day, using its tentacles to reach up and pop open the grate. Cautiously, Petula crept onto Sketchy's back, then stood and peeped through the opening; she found herself looking into a prison cell. A trickle of sunlight filtered in through a barred window, casting striped shadows across the floor.

Petula heard a chain scrape and turned around.

Beatrice was shackled against the wall.

"Mom!" Petula screamed, forgetting herself. She scrambled into the cell and rushed over, throwing her arms around her mother. "You're okay!"

Sir Sap and Sketchy squeezed through the opening and entered the cell as Petula used her fire-zapping spell to melt her mother's shackles. Beatrice flexed her fingers and arms, shaking the feeling back into them, then reached into her pocket and pulled out her deck of picture cards. She shuffled through, showing Petula a series of images in rapid succession: *fwip, fwip, fwip, fwip* . . .

"What is she saying?" Sir Sap asked.

"She's saying we should hurry back to the hotel. The witches will be trying to break inside and steal her perfumier bottles."

Beatrice tugged on her daughter's arm, but Petula resisted. "I'm sorry, Mom, but we can't leave yet. I promised Sir Sap I would help him. His people are starving and the forest sap is the only thing that can help them. We think we know where the queen is hiding it."

Looking troubled, Beatrice pulled out more image cards: *fwip, fwip, fwip* . . .

"No, I'm not crazy," Petula said, "and it's not a bad idea. You go to the hotel and help Warren. I'll keep searching with Sketchy and Sir Sap."

Beatrice nodded but seemed uncertain.

"I'll be okay, Mom. You taught me well. Look!" Petula held out her hand, showing her mother the new rose tattoo. "I caught my first witch—all on my own!"

Beatrice hugged her tightly, with pride shining in her eyes.

Sir Sap looked around in confusion. "Has anyone noticed that we're standing in a prison cell? How in the world are we supposed to get to the caldera?"

Beatrice smiled her mysterious smile and waved her hands in front of the bars. The bone twisted and bent away as though made of taffy.

"Wow," Sir Sap said.

"Cool, right?" Petula grinned. "My mom is pretty great."

Beatrice kissed Petula on the top of her head and then drew a portal that was larger and more powerful than her daughter's.

"Be careful!" Petula called as she stepped through it and disappeared.

Sir Sap crept out of the cell and peered around the corner. "The coast is clear!"

Petula and Sketchy tiptoed after him, past several other cells that sat empty, save for a family of rats sniffing around for food. They followed the long hallway to a flight of stairs, then found themselves approaching the center of the palace. It was a wide chamber, lined with windows and delicate archways knit from bone. Dozens of witches crowded by the windows, peering out at the hotel and cackling with glee.

# "THERE IT IS!"

## "BEATRICE'S BOTTLES ARE HIDDEN SOMEWHERE WITHIN!"

# "OUR SISTERS WILL BE FREED!"

### "LET'S BE THE FIRST TO GREET THEM!"

The witches began clambering out of windows and pushing through doors. Outside, dozens of sap-squatches had also paused in their labor—pulling logs, digging pits, building stone huts—to stare at the spectacle. Compared to Sir Sap, they looked dirty and thin, with matted fur and hollow eyes.

Petula saw the concern in Sir Sap's eyes.

"We'll save them," she assured him.

"At the moment, I'm more concerned about Warren," he said. "He'll have a lot of witches to fend off."

Petula nodded, feeling more anxious than she was willing to admit. "Warren's buying us time," she said.

# "LET'S NOT WASTE IT."

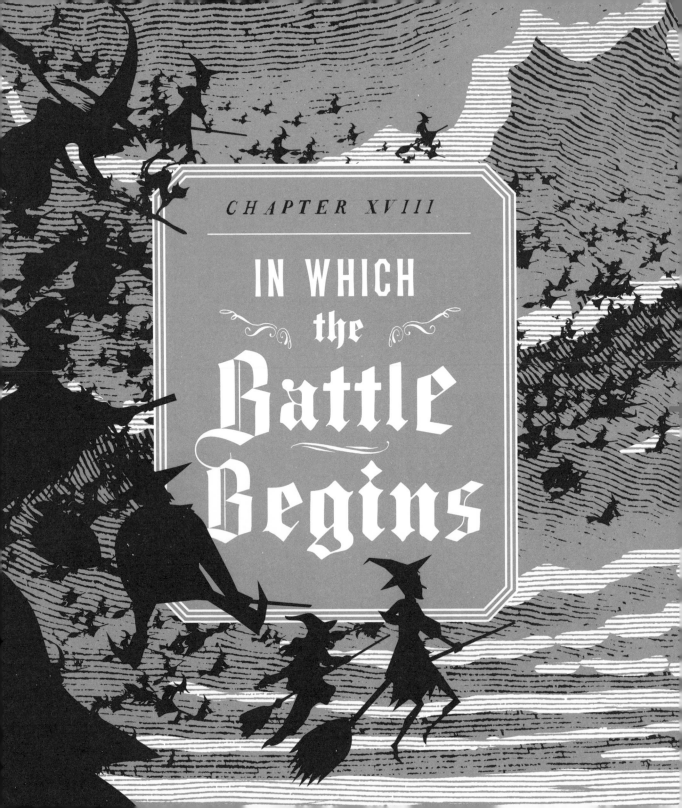

CHAPTER XVIII

IN WHICH
the
Battle
Begins

 arren gripped the controls of the hotel, easing it through the giant pillars that marked the entrance to the Black Caldera. There was nothing but foul black smoke as far as he could see. Still, he pressed on, and as the hotel took another clambering step into the crater, the smoke began to clear. But what it revealed was no better.

All around, witches were swarming like fire ants. Beyond them, Warren could see herds of sap-squatches, who had stopped in the middle of work to gaze in awe at the hotel. They looked miserable, and he hoped Petula and Sir Sap would be able to find their food quickly.

"Everyone ready?" Warren cried. "Because we're going in!"

"Ready!" exclaimed Chef Bunion and Mr. Friggs. Warren had summoned his friends to the control room, along with Uncle Rupert and Mr. Vanderbelly, so that he could make sure everyone was safe. The last thing he needed was someone falling overboard during battle.

"Oh! What thrilling danger we find ourselves in!" cried Mr. Vanderbelly. He had his notebook ready, of course, and seemed delirious with excitement. "Will we succeed in securing the hotel? Or will we be overrun by bloodthirsty witches of a most evil nature? Will I live to tell the tale?"

"Can you please stop asking questions?" Warren implored. "I need to prepare."

"Me, too!" Rupert called from his hammock.

"What are we doing again?" asked Mr. Vanderbelly.

"Don't worry about it," Warren said.

*Thud.* A witch hit the cockpit window, smashing into it like a bug on a windshield. She thwacked her broom and pounded her fists against the glass, trying to break through.

"Oh, my!" Mr. Friggs cried, his dentures nearly spilling from his mouth.

"Everything's fine," Warren assured them. "Beatrice cast a spell on the glass that makes it unbreakable."

He nodded at Beatrice, who had arrived via a portal just a few moments earlier. After a quick explanation using picture cards depicting a lock, a magic wand, and a house, she was now dashing about the hotel, reinforcing all entry points with spells and rendering them witch-proof.

"Let's hope she doesn't miss a spot," Mr. Vanderbelly said.

# THUD.
# THUD.
# THUD.

Warren's attention returned to the window. More witches were slamming into the hotel, beating their broomsticks against the cockpit. Snarling faces pressed against the glass, distorting their already frightening features and blocking Warren's view. He flipped a switch on the control panel and soon a giant windshield wiper scraped across, flinging the witches aside.

"Ha-ha!" Chef laughed. "Atta boy!"

"I'm glad I installed that," Warren admitted. "Pretty handy."

But his smile faded as the building began to shudder. The windshield wiper could do only so much; the thudding grew louder, and it was coming from all sides, along with the occasional zing-blast of a magic spell.

"It's fine," Warren said again. "We're fine!"

Chips of plaster rained down from the ceiling, and the walls gave another sickening shudder. Everyone in the control room huddled a little closer.

"Hurry, Petula," Warren said under his breath.

He wasn't sure how much longer they could last.

Out in the Black Caldera at last, Petula and her companions slipped from hut to hut. Nearly every witch in the basin had stormed the hotel, just as Warren had predicted, leaving all the huts empty. It had the potential to be the perfect plan . . . but only if nothing went wrong.

"The hotel won't last much longer," Sir Sap said, echoing Petula's unspoken fears. "We need to find that sap before it's too late!"

"We're almost there," Petula said. When the coast was clear, they sprinted across the alley to take cover behind the next hut. "When Warren and I were flying here on a broomstick, we saw a building with a ward on the roof. I'll bet you anything that's the hiding place."

Sketchy let out a short tweet and poked a tentacle forward. Sure enough, two witches emerged from a nearby hut, practically tripping over their robes as they hurried to join the excitement at the caldera's entrance.

"Quick!" Petula whispered. Although they barely had time to duck behind a barrel of rocks, the witches didn't even glance their way. After counting to ten, Petula slid around to the back of the hut. A loud crash reverberated against the crater walls: more witches were hitting the hotel. Fear spiked through Petula's veins. They didn't have much time.

"Come on," she beckoned. "Let's forget about being stealthy and make a break for it. On the count of three. One, two—"

But before she could finish, Sir Sap charged ahead, with Sketchy following after; it was all Petula could do to keep up. Out in the open, it took her a moment to get oriented, but off to the right she saw what she was looking for: The building was large, made from stone blocks fitted tightly together and covered with mud and leafy twigs. Whether these were decorations or disguises, Petula couldn't be sure.

"This way!" Petula yelled, and the three of them sprinted off. Sir Sap ran ahead and circled the building.

"There's no door!" he cried.

"We'll need to break in," Petula said. "Grab some rocks!"

First they tried hurling stones at the hut. Then Sir Sap tried using his claws to pry the stones apart, but neither he nor Sketchy was powerful enough to break open the structure. Petula glanced around anxiously. Eventually someone would realize what they were doing. She looked back at the hotel. Its entire surface was crawling with witches. It seemed as though none had yet broken through, but all it would take was one small crack and the whole army would start pouring in. Fortunately, the hotel was strong. Very strong. So strong, in fact—

"That's it!" Petula cried. "We'll get Warren to use the hotel to smash the hut to pieces!"

# "EXCELLENT IDEA!"
## SIR SAP EXCLAIMED.

"I'll portal to him and tell him what to do. You two stand back—and get ready for the sap to flow!"

UEEN CALVINA was reclining on her palanquin, a ghastly-looking bed made from the bones of her less fortunate rivals. Beneath her lumbered four sap-squatches, ready to carry the queen to her new abode.

The hotel was much taller than Calvina had expected; its roof nearly reached the top of the caldera. Soon it would make the most wondrous palace! Now, however, witches were still swarming every square inch of it. Some circled on brooms and batted at windows; others climbed the mighty mechanical legs; still more stomped on the rooftop, searching for a way inside. Hmm, Calvina thought, *why had no one been able to find one?*

She decided it didn't matter. She would succeed where the others had failed. She adjusted her fearsome manticore skull mask and smiled. She knew hundreds, thousands, of catastrophically powerful spells. Which combination would be best? Nothing too destructive, of course. After all, the hotel was to be her new palace, so there was no point in wrecking the place. Perhaps something just harmful enough to scorch the outside, maybe shatter a window or two . . .

With a clang the hotel lurched forward, interrupting Calvina's thoughts. Witches were flung every which way, shaken from the surface like drops of water. The queen sat up in alarm. Her coven sisters were racing past her palanquin. "Where is it going?" she demanded, but no one stopped to answer.

Calvina studied the hotel's path. It was walking around the edge of the caldera, almost as if—no! The hotel was making a beeline for the hut that housed her darkest secret. A secret so important, so powerful, not even her coven sisters knew about it.

"Stop that hotel!" Calvina cried.

"Someone do something! Trip it!"

But the hotel was too big and too strong. Even swarming together in a great cloud, the witches were powerless to stop it.

"Faster!" the queen shrieked. "Get me to that building at once!"

The weary sap-squatches tried to walk faster, but then one stumbled and the queen nearly tumbled from her bed.

"Useless!" Calvina roared. "You lazy, pathetic—"

Her curses were cut short by the crash of a mechanical leg descending on the roof of the warded building. Calvina had designed the building's ward to withstand the most powerful magic . . . but she'd never consid-

ered that it could be physically broken.

Now it was too late. The building lay in ruins, crumbled by the force of the hotel's foot. Within the rubble was a deep pit where the roots of every tree in the forest converged and tangled together. It allowed Calvina to draw sap as easily as turning on a faucet. It was this secret that kept the sap-squatches in her thrall.

But not anymore.

Amber-colored sap shot from the well like a geyser, spraying higher than the caldera's tall walls.

"No!" Calvina screeched. "Not my precious sap!"

Helpless, she clung to the edge of her palanquin as more sap oozed and bubbled into the crater, its sugary scent overpowering the putrid, rotten-egg smells of evil spells that usually hung in the air.

"Sap?" murmured the sap-squatches, repeating the word ever louder as they realized what was happening. "Sap? Sap? Sap?"

"No!" Calvina ordered. "Stay where you are!"

The sap-squatches dropped their hammers and chisels and ropes, abandoning their labor as they rushed to the well. They moved in a feverish frenzy, dancing around and gulping all the sap they could swallow.

"Stop!" Calvina cried. "I forbid you to drink! I'll curse every last one of you! I'll——oof!"

The sap-squatches holding Calvina's palanquin couldn't wait another moment. They dumped her upon the ground and rushed off to join the others.

Calvina staggered to her feet, her mask falling away, and shook her bony fist at the scampering sap-squatches. "Traitors!" she screamed. "Get back here! Don't touch that!" She whirled around to the cloud of witches swarming the hotel. "Sisters! Come help your queen!"

But it was no use. The sap-squatches ignored her. The witches couldn't hear her over the din of destruction. Calvina was alone, deserted and dust covered and positively furious.

"Who did this?" she shrieked. "Who has broken my ward?"

CHAPTER XIX

IN WHICH

A FINAL

Secret

IS

REVEALED

e did it, Warren!" Petula cheered. From inside the cockpit, they had a perfect view of the action below, watching in delight as the hotel's mighty metal feet stomped the sap hut into bits. "The sap-squatches are having a feast! They'll never go hungry again! Look how happy they are!"

It was true: as soon as they bent their muzzles to drink, the sap-squatches seemed to transform. They stood straighter, their eyes shone brighter, their coats glistened in the sun. They flexed their claws and bared their teeth, looking mighty and strong once again.

But Warren was looking elsewhere. Beyond the hut, down on the ground, Queen Calvina was waving madly, a wild expression on her face. Her gown was streaked with dirt. As she screamed into the air, a few witches zoomed down to her side, but it was too late. Stopping the flow of sap was impossible, even with magic. The witches stumbled around, falling face-first into the sticky liquid as they tried to cast their spells. A desperate few tried transforming into their spirit animals, suffusing

the air with the scent of sulfur, and soon the Black Caldera was filled with foxes, boars, bears, cats, weasels, and snakes. But their alternate forms were no better off: sap clung to their fur, dripped off their scales, coated their wings. They were totally and utterly stuck.

"How riveting! How inspiring!" Mr. Vanderbelly dabbed his eyes as he gazed at the scene, taking in all the details. "I have so many articles to write, I scarcely know where to begin!"

Beatrice smiled and shook her head ruefully.

"Ooh, I would love to get my hands on some of that sap," Chef Bunion said. "Imagine all the dishes I could make! Sappy pancakes! Sap fondue! Sap-glazed ham!"

"There won't be a shortage ever again," Warren said. "And there will be plenty of sap to go around for anyone who wants some. Including you, Chef!"

"All this talk of food is making me hungry," Uncle Rupert moaned.

"Look!" Petula said, pointing. "The sap-squatches are winning!"

"Looks like our job here is done," Warren said. "I say we get out of here before any of those witches finds a way to get free. I just have to get Sketchy's attention to let him know we're leaving..."

Beatrice pulled out a card depicting a whirlpool.

"Mom will fetch him," Petula said. "He should be able to fit through her portal."

"Thanks, Beatrice," Warren said, and Beatrice disappeared into a vortex. Not ten seconds later, she reappeared with a happy Sketchy in tow. It shook itself all over like a dog, spraying globules of sap everywhere.

"Mmm!" Rupert licked a drop off his arm. "Yummy!"

"Is that Sir Sap?" Petula asked, squinting. She pointed to the spot where, in the chaos below, a lone sap-squatch was swimming toward the hotel.

"He must be coming to say goodbye," Warren said. "Let's open the hatch!"

Beatrice waved her hand over the hatch set into the floor, dispelling the lock she had placed on it. Petula crouched by the hatch and unfurled the ladder. Down below, the sap-squatch grabbed hold of the ropes and began to climb.

"Wait a second," Warren said. "That doesn't look like Sir Sap."

Indeed, this sap-squatch was smaller than Sir Sap, with delicate features and silkier fur.

"Hello!" Warren said, offering a hand to pull the sap-squatch into the control room. "Welcome to the Warren Hotel!"

"Thank you!" replied the sap-squatch gratefully. "I knew this place was well secured, so I wasn't sure you would allow me inside."

"Are you friends with Sir Sap?" Warren asked.

"Oh, no," the sap-squatch laughed with delight. "I'm his queen!"

"You're the queen of the sap-squatches?" Warren asked in amazement.

"Milady!" Rupert said with an exaggerated bow.

"Yes!" the sap-squatch said. "And I've come to thank you."

"You're welcome!" Warren said, beaming with pride. He had never met royalty before. "I'm just happy your people have their sap back."

"Well, it's good for one thing," the sap-squatch queen said. "Getting this hotel stuck where it belongs."

Stuck? But the hotel wasn't supposed to stay here!

"I beg your pardon?" Warren said.

"After all, it's meant to be my palace." A toothy smile slowly curled over the sap-squatch's face. "You see, I'm not just queen of the sap-squatches. I'm queen of the entire Malwoods!"

In a burst of purple smoke, Queen Calvina appeared where the sap-squatch had stood. Warren gasped. Uncle Rupert shrieked. Even Mr. Vanderbelly was at a loss for words. His pencil slipped from his hand and clattered to the floor.

"Mom!" Petula cried. "Do something!"

Beatrice quickly reached for a bottle, but none was to be found. They had all been taken and smashed by her captors.

"But how?" Warren said. He couldn't believe he'd let Calvina on board. The evil queen merely laughed.

"You poor fools," she drawled. "So stumped when it comes to real magic."

"We're not stumped," Petula said. "Your spirit animal is a sap-squatch!"

"That's correct!" Calvina snarled, and her hands glowed with a mysterious purple energy. "Now I'm afraid I'm going to have to eradicate you all. You've caused a big mess in my home, and it's time to return the favor!"

"Mom, go!" Petula yelled. Beatrice leapt forward, but Calvina shot a purple lightning bolt from her hands, narrowly missing the control panel and cutting a large sizzling dent in the wall.

"Don't be stupid, perfumier!" cackled Calvina. "You're no match for me!"

"Run!" Warren yelled. Uncle Rupert and Mr. Vanderbelly scrambled for the exit, with Chef Bunion and Mr. Friggs and Sketchy fast on their heels. Calvina aimed another crackling blast at Beatrice, throwing her across the room like a rag doll.

"See, now?" Calvina roared. "This is only

a sampling of my power!" She walked over to the stunned Beatrice, her arms glowing and crackling with energy. "Tell me where I can find your collection of perfumier bottles, and I just might spare your friends."

Staggering to her feet, Beatrice spun out of Calvina's way and quickly drew a portal as Petula fired an orange tongue of flames at the queen's knees.

"Ha!" The queen waved her hands in the air, and the entire room froze, as still as glass. "I bind you from all magic!"

With that, Beatrice's portal shattered into a million pieces and Petula's fireball evaporated into smoke and the rose tattoos on Beatrice's body and Petula's hand turned gray like stone.

"My magic!" Petula gasped.

"You think you can fight me?" Calvina crowed. "I have ruled these woods for thousands of years. I am the most powerful witch in the world!"

She shot another dagger of lightning from her palm. Beatrice tried to jump out

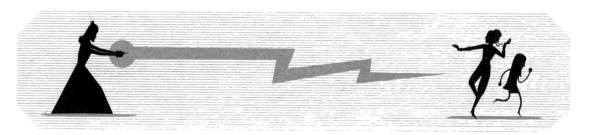

of the way, but the blast hit her foot and she fell to the floor. With a wave of her hands, Calvina caught Beatrice in a cage made of lightning.

"Calvina's too strong," whispered Petula. "Without bottles or magic, Mom can't do anything."

She was right: even raising a hand to the lightning cage caused a massive shock to zap in Beatrice's face. She was trapped.

"Well, we can't give up," Warren said. "Come on!"

He yanked Petula's hand and pulled her out of the control room. The queen, still cackling over the caged Beatrice the Bold, didn't seem to notice the children escaping. Almost.

"Get back here!"

Suddenly a bolt of lightning hissed past Warren's ear.

"Are there any more empty bottles?" Warren asked, puffing hard as he and Petula raced down the hall toward the stairs.

"Yes, on the eighth floor," Petula said. "In my mom's room."

"Think they'll work on the queen?"

"They're better than nothing!"

Warren and Petula took the stairs two at a time and burst into the lobby, where Uncle Rupert, Mr. Friggs, Sketchy, Chef Bunion, and Mr. Vanderbelly were huddled together.

"Go into the ballroom and lock the door!" Warren ordered. "Petula and I will hold her off!"

The others hurried off to do as Warren asked, just as the queen burst into the lobby. "Pesky children!" she said, hurling another bolt of lightning at them. Warren dove for the first cover he could find: a standing mirror. Miraculously, instead of breaking, the shiny surface deflected the blast, and the lightning ricocheted across the room. This time it was Calvina who had to dodge out of the way.

"Ahhh." Warren heard the queen's voice. "Ahh!"

With that, she fell silent. Carefully, slowly, Warren peeped around the mirror's edge. Calvina had lowered her hands and was gazing at her reflection dreamily, almost as if in a trance.

"My, my," she murmured to herself, patting her hair and batting her lashes. "I am beautiful and powerful indeed."

Petula tugged on Warren's jacket and gave him a knowing look. Warren understood. Slowly—and quietly—they crept out from behind the mirror, slinking low along the wall as the queen continued to preen.

Once they reached the staircase, they ran as quickly as they could.

"Eighth floor," Petula whispered.

"Yes," Warren said, "and I've got an idea!"

A few breathless flights of steps later, they were racing down the eighth-floor hallway toward Beatrice's room.

"Wait!" Petula grabbed Warren's arm. The door to the room was ajar. "Something's wrong. This room is always locked." Warren stopped and then heard something. Clinking, scuffling sounds. An intruder!

"But who would—"

He was cut off by a piercing howl from downstairs. Petula's eyes opened wide. "The queen has noticed we're gone," she said.

"We can't turn back now," Warren said, and he leapt forward to the almost-open door and flung it open.

"AHHH!" screamed an oily voice.

Warren frowned. That screaming sounded awfully familiar.

"Sly?" Warren said. "What are you doing here?"

The man was frozen in place, his pockets bulging with jewelry and silver. All the drawers and cabinets were opened and askew.

"Well, kid," Sly said, pocketing another

handful and straightening himself, "I went through a heap of trouble to get onboard this behemoth without being seen, and now I'm just paying myself back for all the damage you did to me and my business."

"But I saved your life!" Warren cried. "If anything, you owe me."

"Po-tay-to, po-tah-to," Sly said, flopping a hand in the air. "The point is, I need to start over. I already checked the hotel safe, but sadly that was empty. So here I am, improvising."

"You're a thief!" Petula cried. She held out a hand to zap him, but then remembered that Calvina had stripped away her powers.

"A handshake, eh?" Sly grabbed her outstretched hand and shook it vigorously. "Call me Sly. Pleasure to make your acquaintance, darling."

Petula drew back as though he were a snake. "Don't touch me! And don't call me 'darling'!"

"My, you have a temper!" Sly said with a chuckle. "I used to have an oil for that. Sly's Soothing Snake Balm. Imbues the user with complete and utter relaxation. A calm mind and spirit. In fact, I used to have a great many oils. But thanks to your little friend here, now I have next to none." He opened his blue satchel—the one he had saved from the quicksand—to demonstrate. "Now if you're in the market for a little something different, I do have—"

Another scream floated up from downstairs, this time loud enough to rattle the door hinges.

"What was that?" Sly said, the color draining from his face.

"You don't want to know," Warren replied.

Meanwhile, Petula had begun to root around the room.

"You messed everything up," she said accusingly. "I can't find my mother's bottles!"

"She's coming," Warren said. "Hurry!"

Petula dug into an overturned drawer.

"I'm looking!" she cried. "You need to stall her! Hold her off!"

*Stall. Stall.* Warren looked around frantically for something he could use, then his gaze fell on Sly's satchel.

"Got it!" Warren snatched the satchel.

"Hey! That's mine!" Sly yelped.

Warren ignored him and tore out into the hallway, just as Calvina reached the eighth-floor landing.

"There you are!" she snarled. "You'll pay for making me run up all those stairs!"

"Why didn't you just make a portal and save yourself the trouble?" Warren asked.

The queen scoffed. "I can't portal to someplace I've never been before, you little fool!"

"Really?" Warren blinked innocently. "I thought you were the most powerful witch in the world."

The queen's violet eyes flashed with fury. "You dare mock me?"

"Not so fast!" Warren said, holding up the satchel. "If you destroy me, you'll also destroy these!" He flipped open the satchel to reveal the amber bottles within.

The queen's eyes widened with hunger. "Give those to me at once!"

"Only if you promise to leave the hotel and never come back!"

"I'm not going to bargain! If you won't give me the bottles, I'll take them by force!"

She raised her glowing hands, poised to cast another spell.

"What are you doing? Those are mine!"

Sly burst into the hallway behind Warren and snatched the satchel from his hands.

"Sly! No!" Warren cried. But Sly had already bolted down the hallway and disappeared around a corner.

"Come back here!" the queen shrieked, and she went racing after Sly to retrieve her prize.

Petula popped out of Beatrice's room, and Warren rushed over.

"Petula, quick," he said. "The satchel—"

"I found one!" Petula held a small bottle aloft. "But just one."

Warren let out a breath. "Hopefully one is all we'll need."

Petula brightened. "Do you have a plan?"

*Sort of,* Warren thought. "Yes," he said bravely, "but we have to get downstairs. Fast!"

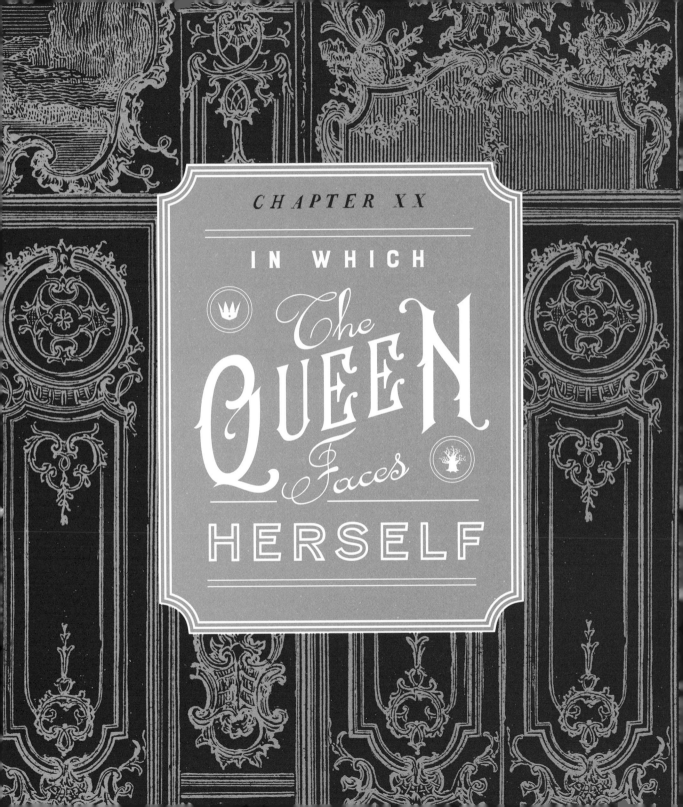

CHAPTER XX

IN WHICH

*The*

QUEEN

*Faces*

HERSELF

arren and Petula burst into the ballroom, where the others were cowering under the long dining table.

"Warren!" Mr. Friggs cried. "Is the queen gone?"

"Not yet," Warren said. "And we're going to need everyone's help to defeat her."

Mr. Vanderbelly was huddled under a chair, reading aloud as he wrote on his notepad: "Young Warren appeared from the trenches of battle to seek our aid. We had no choice but to summon our bravery and hear his plan. How would this saga end?"

"Listen," Warren said. "We don't have much time. Everyone, split up, grab all the mirrors you can find, and bring them to the lobby. Can you do that?"

Chef Bunion, Uncle Rupert, and Mr. Vanderbelly exchanged quizzical looks. Only Mr. Friggs was quick to agree.

"Of course! Come on, everybody, let's join the fight!"

With that, they all rushed to and fro, fetching mirrors from storage closets, powder rooms, and guest bedrooms. Even Uncle Rupert carried a small handheld mirror to further the cause. Soon the lobby was cluttered with looking glasses of

every shape and size: oval vanity mirrors, tall dressing-room mirrors, glimmering decorative mirrors, even a few fun-house mirrors that Chef Bunion had discovered in the back of a closet.

A furious scream reverberated through the hotel, shaking the walls.

"Sounds like Calvina just realized the bottles were fakes," Petula said grimly.

"Thanks for your help, everyone!" Warren said. "Now hurry to the control room and lock yourselves in! Beatrice is there, but she's trapped. See if you can find a way to free her."

"Aye-aye, Cap'n!" Chef Bunion saluted Warren, who blushed. He really did feel like a general!

"I just hope this bottle works," Petula said. "She really is the most powerful witch I've ever encountered. What if somehow she's able to resist it?"

Warren said nothing. They just had to

hope that wasn't true.

Out on the stairs came the sound of harried footsteps. Seconds later, Sly tumbled into the room, a terrified look upon his face. His hair was singed with black soot, and his suit was in tatters. Smoke rose from his lapels, which were burnt to a crisp.

"She's crazy!" he wheezed. "She can have my oil bottles for all I care! Get me offa this hotel!"

"Go downstairs to the control room," Warren said. "There's a trap door and a ladder that will let you out."

"Thanks, kid," Sly said, and then he gave him an odd look. "Say, why aren't you making a break for it? You can't possibly stand up to her. If I were you, I'd get as far away from this place as possible."

"This is my home," Warren said, "and I'm never letting it out of my sight again!"

Sly's mustache twitched. "Suit yourself. I'm outta here!"

The lights in the hotel flickered and dimmed, and a bitter chill coursed through the air.

"I'm tired of these games." Calvina's voice reverberated through the halls. "This ends right now!"

A whirling portal snapped open in the center of the room, and Petula and Warren ducked behind their shield of mirrors just in time. Through the gaps, Warren watched as the queen stepped through the portal and into the lobby. Her entire body was radiant with power, her violet eyes ablaze with brilliant light. Scared as he was, Warren had to admit that she was beautiful—more beautiful than anyone he'd seen in his whole life. He stared transfixed as the queen's light reflected off the myriad mirrors, scattering rainbows across the room.

"Don't look at her directly," Petula whispered, tugging at his arm. "It's like staring at the sun."

Warren blinked, the trance broken, just as the queen noticed the mirrors.

"Oh!" Calvina cried, enthralled by her own reflection. She gazed at herself in one mirror, ran her fingers through her hair, and then turned to gaze in the next. She turned, and smiled, and turned, and curtseyed, and turned again, admiring herself from every possible angle.

"I'm...so beautiful!" she gasped, turning again and then turning some more.

Warren's mirror trap was working—just as he had hoped!

"I can't catch her until she casts a spell," Petula whispered, gripping her bottle.

"Here comes your chance," Warren said, and then he stepped out from his hiding place to face the queen. "You may be beautiful, Your Royal Darkness, but I wonder what your true self looks like."

"What?" The queen whirled around, eyes snapping with rage.

"RORRIM!" WARREN CRIED.

At the sound of the magical word, all the mirrors shimmered. Suddenly the reflections changed from that of a beautiful queen to an ugly, skeletal, twisted creature, its gray skin pocked with scabs and spots and a lashing rat's tail. Its eyes drooped out of their sockets, and its head bristled with tiny horns where hair should be.

"Nooooo!" the queen howled. She turned in circles, desperate to avoid seeing the horrible creature in the mirrors, but everywhere she looked, her true self stared back.

"My beautiful hair! My perfect skin! My captivating eyes!" she cried, raking her hands over her body as she writhed in agony. "This cannot be!"

With a mighty crash, she slammed a fist into the nearest mirror, then the next and the next. Hundreds of shards showered to the ground. But there were too many mirrors to count, and Calvina cut herself on the broken glass. She fell to her knees, rocking in pain.

"No!" she gasped. Her fists tensed and her whole body flickered as she tried to transform into her spirit animal. But at the first whiff of sulfur, Petula was ready. She leapt out from her hiding spot, with bottle uncorked.

"Got you!" Petula cried. Emitting an ear-piercing scream, the queen was sucked toward the bottle. She clawed at the floor, trying to save herself, but the magic was too strong; her body stretched like taffy as the bottle drew her in.

"Careful!" Warren cried.

"I've got it." But Petula's hands were

trembling as she struggled to grip the bottle.

"Here." Warren rushed to her side and placed his hands over hers. "Don't . . . drop . . . it."

With gritted teeth, they both held on tight and watched in morbid fascination as the last wisps of Calvina spiraled away into the belly of the vessel.

And then it was over. The queen was captured!

Petula shoved the cork into the bottle, sealing it for good. "We did it!" she said in elation. "It worked! And look!" She raised her hand, where another rose tattoo formed opposite the first. "My color is back! The binding has been broken!"

"That means Beatrice is free, too!" Warren said.

"Of course!" Petula said.

Broken glass crunched under their feet as they scurried downstairs to the control room.

"We did it, everyone!" Petula cried as they burst in. "The queen is—"

But something held her back—a loose wire on the floor tripped her up and stopped her short. The bottle flew from her hands, spinning madly in the air, arcing toward the ground, sure to shatter if it hit . . .

Suddenly a rubbery tentacle whipped out, catching the bottle mere inches before it crashed to the floor. Sketchy exhaled a series of relieved chirps.

"Phew," Warren breathed. "Good catch, Sketchy!"

"Sorry," Petula blushed, her naturally pale face turning a rosy hue. "I guess I should be a little more careful."

Beatrice, her lightning cage now gone, pulled her daughter into a hug and ruffled her hair affectionately.

"I see the headline now!" Mr. Vanderbelly said, spreading his fingers wide. "Brave Children Save Forest of Sap-Squatches, Defeat Most Powerful Witch in Malwoods!"

"Is it time for lunch yet?" Uncle Rupert complained. "Being so heroic has worked up quite an appetite!"

"I think this calls for a special feast," Chef Bunion said.

"It certainly is cause for celebration," Mr. Friggs piped up. "But I'm afraid we have another problem."

Everyone stopped to stare at the elderly man, who gestured out the window.

By this time, the sap had almost filled the caldera, completely swallowing the village it once contained. In fact, the sap had risen so high that the amber liquid now reached the bottom of the cockpit window.

"The legs," Warren said, his heart sinking fast. "We can't walk through this sticky goo. If we were stuck before, we're even more stuck now."

He pressed his palm against the glass and looked outside. Hundreds of sap-squatches were celebrating, swimming and playing in the sap as the remaining witches looked on miserably.

Warren exhaled and squared his shoulders. A manager had to make the best of any situation, and that's exactly what he was going to do.

"Now that the queen is gone, maybe this isn't such a bad place," Warren said slowly. "Instead of the Black Caldera, we'll call it the . . . the Sap Caldera! The world's first resort for sap-squatches?"

Everyone exchanged worried glances. It didn't seem like an ideal situation, or even a reasonably good one. But then the hotel shifted beneath their feet.

"Earthquake!" Rupert cried. "Was that an earthquake?"

"I'm not sure," Warren said, alarmed. The last thing he needed now was more damage to the hotel.

The control panel lit up, its many buttons blinking and flashing all at once. Outside, a horn bellowed—

# HONK! HONK! HONK!

—as if warning that the hotel was ready to self-destruct. It was so loud, even the sap-squatches could hear it; they stopped playing their games and stared. Then, with a mighty shudder, the Warren Hotel heaved forward.

"We're moving!" Petula cried. "Wait— we're moving?"

With not a moment to waste, Warren rushed to the periscope and turned the crank, trying to glimpse parts of the hotel he couldn't see through the cockpit windows. The river of sap had risen to tremendous heights, and it now carried the hotel out the eastern entrance of the caldera—and straight to the ocean!

"We need to stop," Warren said. "If we walk into the ocean, we'll sink. Quick, somebody help!"

Mr. Friggs scanned the control panel. "There are plenty of ways to stop the hotel from walking," he said, with panic in his voice, "but nothing to keep it from being carried along in a river of sap!"

"You mean . . . ," Chef Bunion began.

"We're doomed!" Rupert howled.

"Doomed!" Mr. Vanderbelly wrote on his notepad.

Everyone screamed and clung to one another as the hotel floated out of the Black Caldera. Trees and trails whipped by the cockpit windows as they cascaded downhill, hurtling toward the ocean like a barrel spilling over a waterfall.

Warren sank to the floor and closed his eyes. After all this time, after all his hard work, his beloved hotel was about to flow out to the ocean and sink like a stone.

# CLANK. CLANK.

Warren opened his eyes.

"What was that?" he said. But his friends just looked at one another and shrugged. *Right,* Warren remembered, *I'm the manager. Answering questions is my job.*

He rushed over to the periscope.

"I—I don't believe it!" he said.

"What is it?" Mr. Friggs cried in alarm. "What do you see?"

"The hotel . . . ," Warren said. "It seems to be . . . transforming!"

"Transforming?" Chef asked.

"Its legs are . . . retracting!"

"Retracting?" Petula repeated.

"Yes! In fact, I think we're turning into—a ship!" Warren squinted again into the periscope. It was extraordinary: at the first touch of seawater, the hotel's enormous appendages had started to draw into the bottom of the building. He saw two plates sliding over the holes, forming a sort of hull.

"Look!" Petula pointed out the windows.

A giant sail emblazoned with the letter "W" had extended from the roof.

Beatrice pulled out a series of picture cards: *Fwip! Fwip! Fwip!*

"Mom says the saltwater must have triggered the transformation," Petula explained.

"What genius!" Mr. Friggs cried, clapping his hands with delight. "Warren the 2nd definitely had some tricks up his sleeve! What a surprise!"

The building wobbled and bobbled some more as it adjusted to the waves, but finally it settled and the hotel-turned-boat sailed upon the ocean. Sketchy let out a shrill whistle and danced about, tentacles wiggling. If there was one thing the creature loved, it was water.

# "WE MADE IT!"

Warren could hardly believe it. Through the cockpit window, he could see curious fish and seahorses flitting by and strands of toffee-like sap being washed away. The building rocked gently from side to side as it was carried along with the tide. Back at the periscope, Warren could see the Malwoods and the volcanic shape of the caldera grow smaller and smaller as they drifted away.

"Warren," Petula said, her eyes shining, "do you realize what this means?"

Warren met her look with a grin. "We can travel anywhere we want!"

"New cuisines to try!" Chef Bunion cried.

"And new adventures to report!" Mr. Vanderbelly added, waving his pencil in the air.

"Oh, dear," Mr. Friggs said, looking as though he might faint.

"Cheer up, Mr. Friggs!" Warren said. "We're not just a world-famous traveling hotel anymore. Now we're a world-famous, world-traveling hotel!"

And with that, he began to sing:

OH HO HO!
WARREN THE 13TH BE MY NAME!
AND TRAV'LING THE GLOBE BE MY CLAIM TO FAME!
NO MONSTER OF LAND, NOR AIR, NOR SEA
WILL EVER SUCCEED IN FRIGHT'NING ME!
FOR I BE CLEVER AND BRAVE AND STRONG!
AND WHEN COURAGE I NEED, I SING THIS SONG!

After a few rounds, the rest of the group joined in, with Sketchy whistling in harmony as the hotel sailed off into the sparkling horizon.

WARREN

MR. FRIGGS

SKETCHY

RUPERT

BEATRICE

CHEF BUNION

PETULA

VANDERBELLY

# *Acknowledgments*

Thank you to all who helped in the making of this book. There are so many people involved. I must start with my wonderful and patient partner, Hanh. She is a saint to have allowed me to do yet another Warren book: you are amazing. I also want to thank all of my friends and family for being so understanding of my crazy schedule during the creation of this book. As to all of those at Quirk, huge thanks as always to Jason Rekulak, who continues to pull off the impossible. This book also would not have been possible without the wonderful efforts of Mary Ellen Wilson, Tim O'Donnell, and the publicity and marketing team of Nicole De Jackmo and Paul Crichton. Last but not least, thank you to all of the fans who have enjoyed staying at the Warren Hotel. We hope you'll come back again.

*—Will*

A second book requires twice the amount of gratitude for all those who helped make it possible. Thanks again to our tireless editor, Jason Rekulak, and all the fantastic people at Quirk whose hands, eyes, and tentacles have helped make this book the best it could be. To all the new writer-friends I have made on this journey, who have pushed me along with words of support and encouragement, thank you! I want to shout out my appreciation to all the new readers, both young and old, who have taken the time to write me, whether by email, Twitter, or post. I love hearing from you! This book is for you. And last but not least, thank you to all the parents, librarians, and teachers who have welcomed us into schools and libraries to share Warren with your kids. It's been a joy getting to meet you all, and I hope there will be more stories and visits to come.

*—Tania*

# WILL STAEHLE

is the creator of Warren the 13th, and is an award-winning designer and illustrator. He grew up reading comics and working summers at his parent's design firm in Wisconsin. He now spends his days designing book covers, posters, and mini-comics, to ensure that he gets as little sleep as possible. He lives in Seattle.

*unusualco.com*

 *@unusualcorp*

# TANIA DEL RIO

is a professional comic book writer
and artist who has spent the past
10 years writing and illustrating,
primarily for a young audience. Her
clients include *Archie Comics, Dark
Horse,* and *Marvel;* she is best known
for her work writing and drawing the
42-issue run of *Sabrina the Teenage
Witch.* She lives in Los Angeles.

*taniadelrio.com*
 *@taniadelrio*